What You Can Do About FOOD POISONING

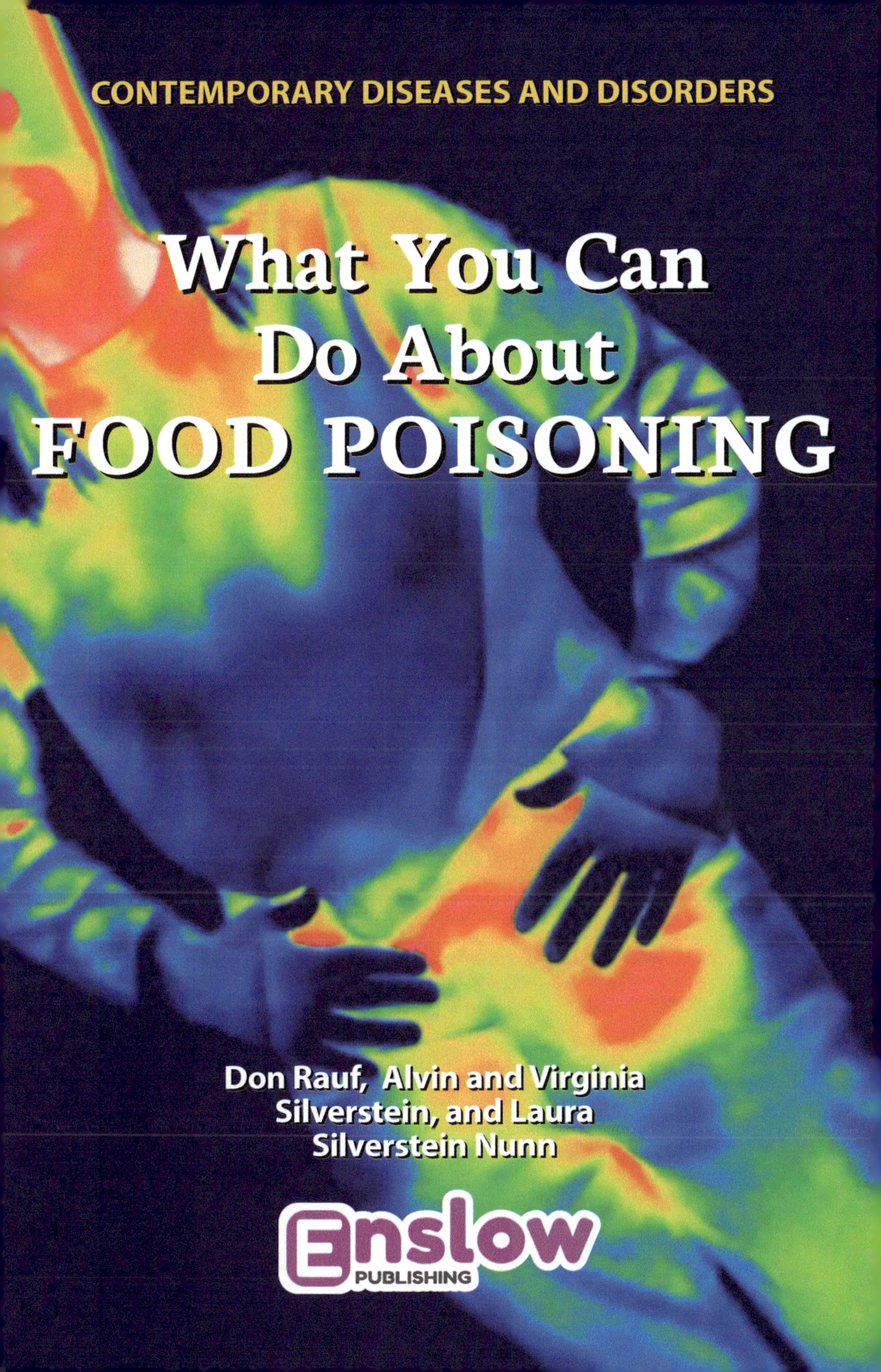

CONTEMPORARY DISEASES AND DISORDERS

What You Can Do About FOOD POISONING

Don Rauf, Alvin and Virginia Silverstein, and Laura Silverstein Nunn

Enslow PUBLISHING

Published in 2016 by Enslow Publishing, LLC
101 W. 23rd Street, Suite 240, New York, NY 10011

Library of Congress Cataloging-in-Publication Data
Rauf, Don.
What you can do about food poisoning / Don Rauf, Alvin and Virginia Silverstein, and Laura Silverstein Nunn.
pages cm. — (Contemporary diseases and disorders)
Audience: Age 12-up.
Audience: Grade 7 to 8.
Summary: "Describes the conditions of food poisoning, the causes, and treatment options"— Provided by publisher.
Includes bibliographical references and index.
ISBN 978-0-7660-7038-7
1. Food poisoning—Juvenile literature. I. Silverstein, Virginia B. II. Silverstein, Alvin. III. Nunn, Laura Silverstein. IV. Title.
RC143.R38 2016
615.9'5293—dc23
2015015551

Printed in the United States of America

To Our Readers: We have done our best to make sure all Web site addresses in this book were active and appropriate when we went to press. However, the author and the publisher have no control over and assume no liability for the material available on those Web sites or on any Web sites they may link to. Any comments or suggestions can be sent by e-mail to customerservice@enslow.com.

Portions of this book originally appeared in the book *The Food Poisoning Update.*

Photo Credits: Ann Ronan Pictures/Print Collector/Hulton Archive/Getty Images, p. 26; © AP Images, pp. 16, 62; Brent Hofacker/Shutterstock.com, p. 29; BSOP/UIG via Getty Images, p. 34; Caiaimage/Robert Daly/OJO+/Getty images, p. 60; cleanfotos/Shutterstock.com, p. 69; Culture Club/Hulton Archive/Getty Images, p. 20; Dan Dalton/Caiaimage/Getty Images, p. 58; Dziewul/Shutterstock.com, p. 77; granata68/Shutterstock.com, p. 73; Hulton Archive/Getty Images, p. 21; Image Point Fr/Shutterstock.com, p. 41; ©iStockphoto/AlbanyPictures, p. 68; ©iStockphoto.com/bhofack2, p. 83; ©iStockphoto/oranhall, p. 90; ©iStockphoto/robeo, p. 86; Jean-Pierre REY/Gamma-Rapho/Getty Images, p. 46; Justin Sullivan/Getty Images, p. 53; Kent Kobersteen/national Geographic Images/Getty Images, p. 64; Margoe Edwards/Shutterstock.com, p. 55; Monica Graff/Getty Images, p. 12; Monkey Business Images/Shutterstock.com, p. 79; NAN728/Shutterstock.com, p. 10; Nonwarit/Shutterstock.com, p. 70; NorGal/Shutterstock.com, p. 85; Olesia Bilkei/Shutterstock.com, p. 81; oliveromg/Shutterstock.com, p. 39; Photo Alto/Isabelle Rozenbaum/Getty Images, p. 25; Radu Bercan/Shutterstock.com, p. 58; Robert-Andre Roszik/EyeEm/etty images, p. 65; Scientifica/Visuals Unlimited/Getty Images, p. 3; Tetra Images/Getty Images, p. 48; Ulrich Baumgarten/Getty Images, p. 32; Valerio Pardi/Shutterstock.com, p. 50; Wavebreakmedia Ltd/Lightwavemedia/Thinkstock, p. 6; www.BillionPhotos.com/Shutterstock.com, p. 43.

Cover Credits: Scientifica/Visuals Unlimited/Getty Images (thermogram of abdominal pain).

Contents

Food poisoning can strike anyone at any time. It can be relatively mild and last just a few hours or it can be serious and require hospitalization.

Food Poisoning at a Glance

WHAT IS IT?

Also called foodborne illness, this sickness is caused by consuming food or drink that has been contaminated with disease-causing germs (bacteria or viruses), parasites, toxins, or chemicals.

WHO GETS IT?

Anyone can get it, both males and females of any ethnic group. The Centers for Disease Control and Prevention (CDC) estimates that one in six Americans (forty-eight million) get food poisoning every year. Young children, pregnant women, the elderly, and people with weakened immune systems are the most vulnerable to the illness.

WHAT ARE THE SYMPTOMS?

Food poisoning can have many different causes, so symptoms can vary greatly. Common symptoms include nausea, abdominal pain, vomiting, diarrhea, fever, headache, and tiredness. Food poisoning can be very serious and result in death.

Symptoms usually appear twelve to seventy-two hours after eating contaminated food.

HOW IS IT TREATED?

In most cases, patients require bed rest and replacing lost fluids and electrolytes (nutrients and minerals). More serious cases may need medical attention.

HOW CAN IT BE PREVENTED?

Wash hands and food surfaces with soap and water before and after handling fresh meat, poultry, or fish, and after using the bathroom. Cook foods to safe temperatures (especially meat, poultry, fish, and eggs). Keep perishable foods refrigerated.

1 Chapter

When Eating Is Risky Business

People take cruises expecting to have relaxing vacations. They want to enjoy various tourist sites as well as the diversions, accommodations, and good food aboard a cruise ship. That's exactly what Jim and Sharon* sought when they booked a cruise in Europe to celebrate Sharon's birthday. They may have feared getting a little seasick, but they never thought they'd get food poisoning.

The couple set sail for a two-week summer cruise aboard the MS *Independence of the Seas*. They enjoyed being aboard the boat, but on their very first night, they noticed that their dinner was served cold. They had a few bites but they had to send the food back to the kitchen. Over the next several days, they tried to unwind and celebrate Sharon's birthday, but the food kept disappointing them. They received more cold dinners. The milk was curdled. The yogurt didn't taste quite right. Two days before the end of their trip, both Jim and Sharon got very ill with nausea, vomiting and diarrhea. The food had not

**Not their real names*

A cruise can be a great way to have fun and see new places. Unfortunately, the crowded conditions aboard the ship may contribute to the spread of foodborne illnesses.

been stored and prepared properly and the couple were now sick with food poisoning. The romantic cruise had turned into a nightmare at sea.[1]

While most cruise ship passengers enjoy great food, free of contaminants, there have been several cases of foodborne illness aboard ships. In January of 2014, about six hundred people fell ill on a Royal Caribbean cruise out of New Jersey with what appeared to be food-related sickness. One traveler described how he had an upset stomach and vomiting that lasted all night and into the morning.[2] A year later in February 2015, another Royal Caribbean cruise was cut short when two hundred passengers fell ill. The ship, which started in Baltimore, had to turn around. In both cases, health experts suspected the

Norovirus was to blame.[3] The Centers for Disease Control and Prevention (CDC) has labeled the Norovirus as the most common cause of foodborne-disease outbreaks in the United States.[4] The Norovirus can thrive on food, water, and surfaces and it's easily transmitted from person to person. Similar cases of Norovirus have been reported on a 2014 cruise out of Los Angeles, infecting about three dozen passengers. That same year, two hundred people aboard a Carnival cruise in New Zealand were stricken with the disease. In all cases, passengers were encouraged to stay in their rooms so as not to spread the illness. The ship staff intensely wiped down all surfaces with disinfectant.

Food illnesses are certainly not limited to cruise ships, but these vessels seem to get more than their fair share of stomach-cramping sickness. The CDC recorded fourteen gastrointestinal outbreaks on cruise ships in 2010 and 2011, sixteen in 2012, and nine in 2013. Some experts say the close quarters are to blame. Some illnesses start with food, then are passed along by human contact or contact with materials. On a ship, passengers are continuously touching railings, bathroom doors, buffet tables and other surfaces. With a lot of people living close together on a ship, it can almost become a breeding tank for disease. When people are in a confined space, they are very susceptible to an infection. Cruise ships may also stop at locations that are known to have food and water with contaminants. Sometimes, one person can pick up an illness with a port excursion to a local eatery. He or she brings it back on the ship and can light a fuse that can send explosive sickness to many of the passengers.

Everybody gets stomachaches at one time or another. Sometimes they are caused by eating too much. Some people get them when they eat a food that "doesn't agree with them." But when two or more people are having stomach problems after eating the same food, it could be a sign of food poisoning.

Once a foodborne illness is found on a cruise ship, the entire ship must be cleaned and disinfected. This worker is part of a cleaning crew hired after food poisoning affected a cruise ship in 2003.

Food poisoning is an illness that happens when people consume food or drink that has been contaminated with harmful chemicals or disease-causing creatures, such as bacteria, viruses, or parasites. Some bacteria send out toxins (poisons) that can make food go bad. Others produce toxins while they are multiplying in a person's body. Some foods, such as certain kinds of mushrooms and fish, naturally contain poisonous chemicals that can make people sick.

Food poisoning is an illness that happens when people consume food or drink that has been contaminated with harmful chemicals or disease-causing creatures, such as bacteria, viruses, or parasites.

Medical experts often use the term *foodborne illness* for cases of food poisoning, especially those caused by bacteria and other microorganisms. Although the food supply in the United States is one of the safest in the world, food poisoning is fairly common. According to the CDC, every year an estimated forty-eight million Americans get sick from something they ate. That's about one in six citizens. Nearly 128,000 of them need to be hospitalized, and more than three thousand die from eating contaminated food.[5]

Most cases of food poisoning are mild and will go away after a couple of days. For this reason, many people do not seek medical help. Sometimes, however, the illness can last for days, even weeks. When symptoms become more serious, a trip to the hospital is necessary. In some very rare cases, food poisoning may lead to death.

CELEBRITY FOOD POISONING[6]

No one is immune to food poisoning. Even celebrities have been brought down by contaminated food. Here are a few famous folks who suffered from foodborne illnesses during 2011 and 2012.

Country star Miranda Lambert tweeted that she had a "near death experience" when she came down with a severe case of food poisoning.

George Clooney and his entire dinner party were brought down by food gone foul at a restaurant in Italy.

William Shatner boldly went through with his one-man show in New York but struggled on opening night with a bout of food poisoning.

Sir Elton John canceled two shows in Las Vegas rocked by food gone rotten. As one gossip paper said: "Goodbye, Yellow Brick Road; Hello, Porcelain Throne."

Selena Gomez suffered such tummy turmoil after an appearance on The Tonight Show *that she was rushed to the hospital with severe headache and nausea. She canceled her show that night at the Santa Monica Pier.*

Rapper DMX headed to the hospital after eating suspicious shrimp.

Michael Winner, a restaurant critic in England, made his own steak tartare (raw chopped steak) only to be stricken with E. coli *poisoning.*

Aerosmith singer Steve Tyler collapsed after becoming dehydrated with food poisoning.

Brazilian soccer legend Socrates died after eating infected beef stroganoff. He went into septic shock (a severe condition of life-threatening low blood pressure resulting from an overwhelming infection). He also was in a coma before dying.

2 Chapter

Food Poisoning Through the Ages

There is no way to guarantee that the food we eat is completely safe. However, by following a number of food safety guidelines, we can greatly reduce the chances of getting food poisoning. Mary Mallon emigrated from Ireland to the United States in the 1880s. A hard worker, Mary gradually established herself as a respected chef. Wealthy New York families regularly employed her. But because of an unfortunate twist of fate, Mary became known as the spreader of a deadly disease called typhoid, and in the pages of history, she became known as Typhoid Mary.

Typhoid is a foodborne illness caused by bacteria in the *Salmonella* family. Like many food poisoning sicknesses, the bacteria can be transmitted through human contact. The bacteria inflame the small and large intestine. Symptoms include high fever, loss of appetite, headache, diarrhea, sore throat, abdominal pain, and extreme tiredness. In the worst cases, it can lead to death. Antibiotics can cure the disease today, but at the turn of the century, there was no cure for typhoid.

Marry Mallon, who became known as Typhoid Mary, was quarantined in this isolated cottage on North Brother Island in New York's East River from 1907 to1910 and again from 1915 until her death in 1938.

In the summer of 1906, prominent banker Charles Henry Warren hired Mary to be the cook at his family's summer vacation home in Oyster Bay, Long Island. On August 27, one of Warren's daughter's cam down with typhoid fever. Within a short time, six out of eleven people in the household had come down with the disease, including Warren's wife, another daughter, and two housemaids.

The source of the outbreak at the Warren house was a mystery at first. At that time in American history, typhoid was fairly common. In 1906 New York City had 3,467 cases, 639 ending in death. Warren wanted to find the source of the disease and clear up the problem to assure that no more people would get sick.

That winter, George Soper, a sanitary engineer who had experience with typhoid outbreaks, was asked to investigate. He tested the water sources but did not find any disease-causing organisms. He then focused on the cook, Mary Mallon, whose hiring corresponded with the disease outbreak.

By that time, Mallon was no longer working for the Warrens; she had left them about three weeks after the typhoid started to claim its victims. Soper discovered that among the seven families for whom Mallon had worked between 1900 and 1907, twenty-two people had become ill with typhoid fever. Soper was convinced he was on the right track. The next thing he needed to do was to get samples of Mallon's blood and stool (feces) to prove that she had spread the disease.

Mallon resisted being tested at first. In fact, when Soper asked if she would provide samples of urine, feces and blood, she chased Soper away with a carving fork. With the help of police, Mallon was taken to the Willard Parker Hospital in New York, where samples of her blood and stool were finally collected. Tests of the samples showed typhoid bacteria in her stool. It was clear that Mallon was a carrier—she had most likely spread typhoid bacteria to other people even though she did not have any symptoms. Not everyone with typhoid becomes very ill. It is possible that Mallon might have had a mild case of typhoid and thought she had a touch of the flu. After she recovered, some typhoid bacteria remained in her body and continued to come out in her stool. She most likely spread the disease when she cooked for people with unwashed hands after going to the bathroom. Unfortunately, no one at the time explained all the facts to Mary Mallon, and she continued to feel that she was being falsely accused. (Some of her defenders believe that some of the typhoid could very well have been spread by others.)

Mallon was kept under house arrest in an isolated cottage for the next three years without having had a trial. By this time, people were calling her Typhoid Mary. The sensationalist press fueled her image as a carrier of deadly disease—one paper showed an illustration of her cooking eggs, but the eggs were shown to be skulls. In 1910 a new health commissioner decided to give Mallon her freedom as long as she agreed not to work as a cook again. Mallon agreed and was released.

In January 1915 another typhoid outbreak hit Manhattan. Twenty-five people got sick, and two of them died. Evidence pointed to a cook named Mrs. Brown—who turned out to be Mary Mallon, using a fake name. Mallon never believed that she was spreading the disease. She was sent back into isolation, where she stayed for the next twenty-three years. All in all, Typhoid Mary was linked to about fifty cases of typhoid fever; three of the patients died.[1,2]

THE HISTORY OF FOOD SAFETY

Food safety has been a major concern for humans throughout history—since long before Mary Mallon's time. In ancient times, people often got sick from eating spoiled food. Early on, they learned that animals killed for food had to be eaten right away before the meat went "bad." Soon people figured out how

This 1909 illustration of Typhoid Mary shows her breaking skulls into a pan instead of eggs. She is presumed to have infected over fifty people during her career as a cook.

FOOD TASTERS

During the Middle Ages (about AD 500 to 1500), poisons hidden in food were commonly used as a weapon. To prevent assassination attempts on an important person, such as an emperor or king, it was common for Royal Courts to use "food tasters"—people who ate a sample of the food first to make sure it was not poisoned. If the food taster survived, then the food was safe to eat. However, this test was not very useful for slow-acting poisons, which take a long time to do their damage.

to use nature's tools to preserve food so that they could eat it at a later time. For example, in cold climates, meat was packed in ice to keep it frozen. In warm climates, foods were dried in the sun. During the Middle Ages, the Romans built "still houses" (much like greenhouses) in which they could dry fruits, vegetables, and herbs in areas where the sun was not strong enough for drying.

In the 1600s, wealthy Americans and food sellers such as butchers had icehouses built to store their ice and to keep their food frozen. In the early 1800s, the icebox was invented, and people could then store food inside their home. However, people with iceboxes had to receive regular deliveries of ice to

Before refrigerators were common in most households, families relied on a delivery of ice for their icebox. This photo was taken in 1926.

keep their icebox cold. In the late 1800s, the first mechanical refrigerator was invented. It had its own built-in cooling system, which eliminated the need for ice deliveries. By the early 1930s, refrigerators had become common in American homes.

An important breakthrough in food preservation took place in the 1790s. Nicolas Appert, a French confectioner, discovered that food heated and sealed in airtight glass bottles could be stored safely for days, months, or even years. Around 1806 Appert tested his discovery on Napoléon Bonaparte's French army. It was not uncommon for men in the military to get sick, and even die, from spoiled food. Appert was able to supply them with a wide variety of foods, including meat, vegetables, fruit, and milk. The test was a success—no one got sick.

In 1810 Englishman Peter Durand made an important change in Appert's methods: He developed a process that sealed food into unbreakable metal containers—cans. The first commercial canning factory was set up in England in 1813. The cans were lighter than glass bottles, easier to seal, and less likely to get damaged during storage and transportation.

Canning has proved to be a successful method of protecting and preserving food. If the food is not heated high enough or long enough during the canning process, however, canning does not protect against one important form of food poisoning: botulism.

Canning has proved to be a successful method of protecting and preserving food.

SAUSAGES AND BOTULISM

Botulism is the deadliest form of food poisoning in history. The first reported outbreak was in 1793, in Wildbad, Germany. It affected thirteen people, killing six of them, after they ate

CHOLERA ALONG THE THAMES

When a cholera outbreak hit London in 1854, health officials blamed it on "bad air." It was a common belief that this disease affected only poor people and was brought on by unclean conditions in overpopulated areas. Throughout history, cholera had been a devastating disease, causing severe diarrhea, dehydration (serious water loss), fever, and often death.

John Snow, a physician, started his own investigation into the cholera outbreak. After mapping out each cholera case, Snow noticed that most of the cases—with about five hundred deaths in just ten days—occurred in one neighborhood.[3] *These people had one main thing in common: They all got their water from the Broad Street pump. It seemed obvious to Snow that the water from the Broad Street pump was somehow infecting people with cholera.*

Snow convinced local officials to remove the handle from the Broad Street pump. This forced the residents to get their water from another pump. The number of cholera cases dropped immediately. Snow later uncovered the source of the problem. Apparently, the water company that supplied the Broad Street pump got their supply from the Thames River, which had been heavily polluted with raw sewage.

John Snow did not show that germs caused cholera, but he did show how quickly disease can spread through a population.

contaminated blood sausage. The sausage was made by filling a pig's intestines with meat and blood, and then boiling it in water. After that, it was stored at room temperature. As more and more people fell ill, a local doctor, Justinius Kerner, decided to do his own research into this "sausage poisoning," as he called it. In 1829 he published a report describing 230 cases, in which most of the patients had eaten sausage. Kerner wrote about the sausage poison, which had devastating effects on the nervous system. Patients had blurred vision and dry mouth; it was hard for them to swallow and to speak clearly. They suffered from muscle weakness, which developed into paralysis. In severe cases, the poison paralyzed the respiratory muscles, making it hard to breathe and ultimately leading to death.

Sausage poisoning was named botulism, from *botulus*, which is Latin for "sausage." Although Kerner made a detailed study of the disease, he was not able to determine exactly what caused it. At that time, people did not realize that invisible germs could cause diseases.

BACTERIA LEADS TO DISEASE

It was not until the mid-1800s that a link was made between bacteria and disease. In 1857 French chemist Louis Pasteur showed that milk turned sour because microorganisms were growing in it. Starting in the early 1860s, Pasteur conducted experiments in which he used heat to kill the harmful microorganisms in beer and wine. He found that the wine-spoiling creatures could be destroyed by heating the wine to 135°F (57°C). Harmful microorganisms in milk were destroyed when the milk was heated to 161°F (72°C). This process, now called pasteurization, was named after Louis Pasteur. By 1917 most major American cities had laws that required milk to be pasteurized.

In 1878 Louis Pasteur published a paper detailing his "germ theory" of disease. He proposed that many diseases are caused by tiny microorganisms, like those that grow in milk and wine. Pasteur's discoveries made a huge impact on the medical community. However, he was not able to identify the germs that caused the various diseases, as he had hoped to do. German physician Robert Koch, on the other hand, developed methods for growing bacteria in a laboratory. He used staining techniques that allowed him to identify germs. He also laid out specific procedures that had to be followed in order to prove that certain bacteria caused certain diseases. In 1876 Koch identified the first bacterium to be linked to a particular disease—anthrax. Anthrax is a disease that usually affects animals, but it can be transmitted to humans. In 1882 he discovered the bacterium that causes tuberculosis. Then in

The first known outbreak of botulism occurred in 1793 as a result of eating blood sausage.

Scientist Louis Pasteur discovered that the bacteria in milk and wine could be killed by heating them to a certain temperature. That method is now called *pasteurization*.

1883, while he was in Egypt investigating a cholera outbreak, he discovered the bacterium that causes the foodborne illness cholera.

The linking of germs with diseases also made it possible to determine the cause of botulism. In 1895 a group of musicians played at a funeral in Belgium. Within a day or two, twenty-three of the thirty-four musicians became seriously ill. They had double vision, difficulty swallowing, and muscle paralysis. Three of them died. A Belgian doctor, Emile van Ermengem, investigated the outbreak and learned that the musicians had eaten a meal of pickled and smoked ham after the funeral. Van Ermengem fed some of the ham to laboratory animals, and they came down with the same symptoms as the musicians. Then he isolated bacteria from samples of the ham and from the victims. Van Ermengem continued to study these bacteria, which are now known as *Clostridium botulinum*. He found that these microorganisms grow and multiply only under oxygen-free conditions, such as in a sausage (covered by an airtight casing) or in canned foods. As they grow, the bacteria produce a powerful toxin (poison), which remains in the food. Van Ermengem advised that food be cooked properly, and any food that looks or smells bad should be thrown out. This is still good advice today.

3 Chapter

Understanding Food Poisoning

You know the old saying, "An apple a day keeps the doctor away." Well, in the fall of 2014, apples did just the opposite. Cathy Jones of Albuquerque, New Mexico, was pregnant in October of that year. A family friend bought her a treat of caramel apples. What harm could an apple do? In fact, it would satisfy her sweet cravings and give her some "healthy" fruit at the same time. Soon after eating it, however, she was stricken with chills, fever, diarrhea, and muscle aches. She felt so sick she went to the local hospital. There she learned that she had a bacterial infection called listeriosis, commonly caused by the foodborne bacteria *Listeria*. Pregnant women in their last trimester are especially susceptible to the disease, as well as newborns and those whose immune systems are weakened.

Sick with this food poisoning, Cathy delivered her baby one day after being admitted to the hospital. The boy was born several months before his due date. Doctors ran tests on the

Contaminated apples were the cause of a *Listeria* outbreak in 2014 and 2015.

child and found that he too had the potentially deadly illness. The baby had to remain in intensive care for four weeks, but fortunately he survived.

The CDC reported that thirty-five people from twelve states were infected with *Listeria* during this outbreak. The bacteria were linked to commercially produced, prepackaged whole caramel apples. The illness contributed to at least three deaths. Eleven cases of listeriosis were in pregnant women and one pregnant mother lost her baby because of the food poisoning. The disease was eventually traced to an apple supplier in California that recalled its Granny Smith and Gala apples. Once the source of the disease was identified, the spread of the *Listeria* was contained and the CDC said that the outbreak appeared to be over as of February 2015.

Foods like these caramel apples often seem harmless. But even items sold by established grocery chains and restaurants can become contaminated. Every year, stories similar to the one like this *Listeria* outbreak with apples make headlines. And major companies are not immune.[1]

In 1993 one of the most infamous food poisonings occurred when the food chain Jack in the Box began selling its Monster Burgers, which sold under the unfortunate tag line: "So good, it's scary."

Nine-year-old Brianne Kiner loved cheeseburgers. In January of that year, Brianne and her family enjoyed a meal of burgers from a Jack in the Box near her home in Seattle. A few days later, she and her sister, Karin, started to develop flu-like symptoms and diarrhea. Karin started to feel better, but Brianne's illness got worse. She had painful abdominal cramps, and her diarrhea became bloody. Brianne's parents took her to the hospital.

One by one, her major organs failed and within a week she had slipped into a coma. For over forty days, she remained unconscious. Doctors warned her parents several times that they did not think she would survive. Brianne suffered three strokes, ten thousand seizures, failure of every major organ, brain damage, and muscle atrophy.

After nearly six weeks, Brianne woke up from her coma and continued to get stronger. Her large intestine, however, was so damaged that doctors had to remove much of it. Her pancreas was also damaged, making it difficult for her body to use sugar properly, so she had to take medicine for diabetes. She needed to relearn many things she had taken for granted—walking, talking, and even chewing.

Health officials discovered that Brianne's sickness was caused by undercooked burgers from Jack in the Box. As it turned out, the burgers contained a dangerous type of bacteria called *Escherichia coli* O157:H7, or *E. coli* O157:H7 for short. *E. coli* can be found in the intestines of warm-blooded animals. Most strains of *E. coli* are not harmful, but this particular one—*E. coli* O157:H7—produces a powerful toxin that can cause serious damage to the intestine, kidneys, and other important organs.

A total of 623 people fell ill with *E. coli* that was traced to the Jack in the Box burgers. Four children eventually died from the infection. Jack in the Box had been undercooking the meat as well. Experts say that if the chain had cooked the meat to standard temperature, it could have killed the *E. coli* bacteria in the patties.[2]

Before this outbreak, few people knew much about *E. coli.* That changed when news about the Jack in the Box *E. coli* poisoning made it to newspapers and TV all over the country.

As an adult, Brianne still has health problems stemming from the *E. coli* infection. But she is a strong person with a positive attitude. Despite what she has been through, she still loves to eat hamburgers, but now she's a little more cautious. "I just make sure the burgers I eat are thoroughly cooked," she explains.[3]

HOW FOOD CAUSES ILLNESS

Food is an important part of our everyday lives. It provides the body cells with important nutrients we need to live. Sometimes, however, the food we eat can make us sick. Every year, millions of Americans get sick from something they have eaten. In fact, many people will have some kind of food poisoning a number of times during their lifetime.

Food poisoning is an illness caused by contaminated food or drink. Food is said to be contaminated if it has been in contact with something harmful. It may contain certain bacteria, viruses, parasites, molds, yeasts, their toxins, or toxins found in the food itself.

Most cases of food poisoning are caused by microorganisms. Under the right conditions—a warm, moist environment with plenty of food—germs can grow and multiply. Bacteria

Hamburgers can make a person sick if the meat contains bacteria and is not cooked thoroughly.

can grow quickly in food if it is left out at room temperature for too long. Some bacteria produce toxins as they grow in food. When people eat the food, the toxins may make them sick. Some germs make people sick after they multiply inside the body. People often don't realize that food has gone bad because many bacteria do not make food smell or look different.

Food poisoning is an illness caused by contaminated food or drink. It may contain certain bacteria, viruses, parasites, molds, yeasts, their toxins, or toxins found in the food itself.

Foods that are most likely to be contaminated include poultry (chicken, duck, turkey), meats (beef, pork, lamb), seafood (fish, oysters, shrimp), eggs, and dairy products (milk, cheese, yogurt). Food manufacturers use various methods to keep foods free of harmful germs or to prevent them from multiplying. Milk is pasteurized (heated briefly to a high temperature, then rapidly cooled) to kill bacteria. Deep-freezing and drying foods prevent the growth of germs.

Canned foods can be kept safely for a long time because most bacteria cannot grow and multiply without air. However, the deadliest form of food poisoning, botulism, is caused by a type of bacterium that can grow without air. Normally, bacteria are killed by the heat and high pressures of the canning process. If canning is not done properly, however, they can grow and multiply and produce a very deadly toxin.

People may unknowingly buy foods that do contain bacteria. Vegetables that are eaten raw, such as lettuce, may still carry bacteria from the soil in which they were grown. More bacteria may have been added by people who handled them during washing and packing. Washing raw vegetables thoroughly can help get rid of most of the bacteria.

Meats and poultry sold in the supermarket may contain bacteria as well. Eggs may also be contaminated, although the risk is relatively low. The bacteria in meats and other foods that are cooked do not usually cause illness because high temperatures kill bacteria. Freezing food can keep bacteria from growing and multiplying—but it does not kill them. The bacteria will become active again once the food is thawed. Keeping food refrigerated may help to keep most bacteria from growing, but the best way to destroy the bacteria is by cooking the food thoroughly.

Foods that are most likely to be contaminated include poultry, meats, seafood, eggs, and dairy products.

The CDC says that consumers can reduce their risk for foodborne illness by following safe food-handling and preparation recommendations.[4] For example, food handlers need to

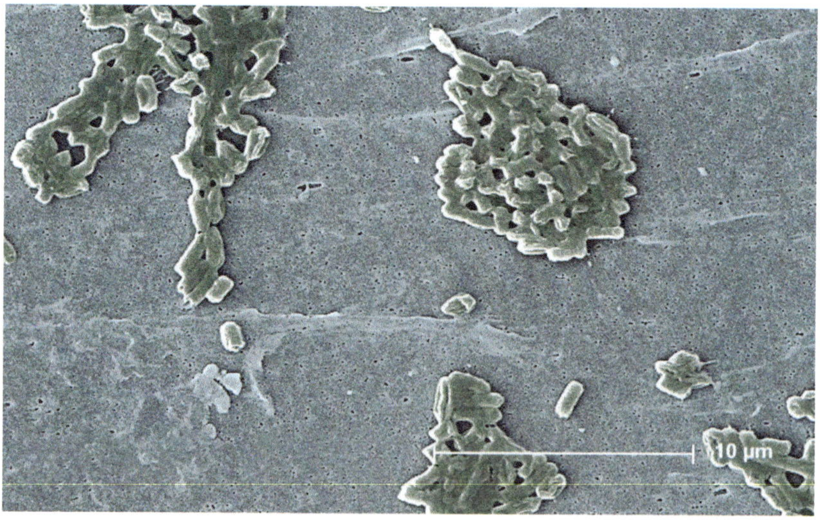

E. coli in contaminated water is shown under a microscope. Microorganisms like *E. coli* can cause food poisoning if foods or drinks are not prepared and stored correctly.

HOW BACTERIA GROW SO FAST

When a person eats food contaminated with disease-causing bacteria, the bacteria can multiply quickly inside the body. Each bacterium reproduces by dividing into two smaller bacteria. Each offspring grows and then divides, too. When the temperature is just right and there is plenty of food, one bacterium can divide into two bacteria every twenty to thirty minutes. A few bacteria would not be enough to make a person feel ill, but after a few hours, just one germ could multiply into millions!

wash their hands after going to the bathroom. (Bacteria are found in a person's feces.) An infected person can spread germs to other people who may prepare a meal for their family or for people in a restaurant. Remember that Typhoid Mary spread the typhoid bacterium to a number of people when she worked as a cook. She was a carrier—she had no symptoms of the disease, but she could pass the germ on to others.

The CDC says that consumers can reduce their risk for foodborne illness by following safe food-handling and preparation recommendations.

Bacteria that normally live in the nose and throat or on the skin may cause trouble if they contaminate food and then multiply when the food is left at room temperature. A 2014 study from the Center for Science in the Public Interest found that a person is twice as likely to get food poisoning dining out at a restaurant than cooking at home. Foodborne illnesses, however, may be declining—the study showed a 42 percent drop in food poisonings from 2002 to 2011.[5]

HOW DOES FOOD POISONING AFFECT THE BODY?

Even if you eat contaminated food, you are not guaranteed to get food poisoning. Whether or not you get sick depends on a number of things: your age, how much of the contaminated food you ate, and how strong your immune system is. The immune system includes various cells and chemicals that help defend the body against germs and other foreign substances. Normally, the immune system does a good job of protecting the body from harmful invaders. If it didn't, you would get sick much more often.

Let's say you eat some chicken that is contaminated with *Salmonella* bacteria. Taking just one bite can carry thousands of bacteria into your body. Once they are swallowed, the bacteria travel to the stomach, where most of them are killed by the stomach acid there. However, some bacteria survive the acid bath. They are sent on to the intestines by the muscular contractions that push food through the digestive tract. In the intestines, the bacteria find everything they need to grow and multiply—warmth, moisture, and plenty of food. They head toward the lining of the intestines. The bacteria invade cells on the surface and start to multiply.

Whether or not you get sick depends on a number of things: your age, how much of the contaminated food you ate, and how strong your immune system is.

Within a few hours, the infected cells in the intestinal lining start to die. Soon the bacteria spread to nearby cells and infect them, too. In less than eight hours, there may be a million *Salmonella* bacteria roaming inside your intestines. Their population continues to grow, doubling in as little as twenty to thirty minutes.

TYPES OF BACTERIA THAT MAY CAUSE FOOD POISONING

Type of Bacterium	How It Spreads	Symptoms
Campylobacter	*Untreated drinking water; infected pets; unpasteurized milk; contaminated raw or undercooked meat, poultry, or shellfish*	*Diarrhea (possibly bloody), cramps, fever, headache*
Clostridium botulinum	*Contaminated canned foods or sausages*	*Double vision, droopy eyelids; trouble speaking, swallowing, or breathing; can be deadly if not treated*
Escherichia coli O157:H7	*Contaminated drinking water, raw or undercooked ground beef, unpasteurized milk, salad greens (lettuces)*	*Severe abdominal cramps, diarrhea (often bloody), nausea, vomiting, fever; may need hospitalization*
Listeria	*Untreated drinking water, unpasteurized milk and other dairy products, contaminated undercooked meat and seafood, contaminated cold cuts, raw vegetables fertilized with infected manure*	*Adults: fever, chills, muscle aches, nausea, diarrhea* *Infants: vomiting, will not drink, breathing difficulty*
Salmonella	*Eating or touching contaminated undercooked chicken, eggs, or beef; infected pets*	*Nausea, fever, stomach cramps, diarrhea, vomiting*
Shigella	*Contaminated poultry, milk and other dairy products, salad greens; often spread due to poor sanitary practices*	*Abdominal pain, fever, sometimes vomiting, mucus in stool*

You may not realize that all this is going on, but your immune system soon finds out. When the body cells are damaged, they send out chemicals that alert the body's defenders to the danger. Some of these chemicals cause fluid to leak out of the blood vessels and into the body tissues, making them swell. The process is called inflammation. Other chemicals produced by damaged cells alert white blood cells, the body's main line of defense.

White blood cells are jelly-like blobs that can swim freely through the blood. They can also move easily through inflamed, fluid-filled tissues. Some of the white blood cells make chemical weapons called antibodies that kill germs or stop them from multiplying. Other white cells swarm over the germs and gobble them up. However, some white blood cells are killed by poisons from the *Salmonella* bacteria they have eaten.

As the bacteria kill more and more cells, you start to feel sick. The muscles in your stomach wall start to contract (tighten) so much that it hurts. The intestines contract, too, but instead of sending the food along its usual route, they may squeeze some of it back into the stomach. Meanwhile, messages are sent along nerves from the throat and stomach to a special vomiting center in your brain. You begin to feel nauseated, "sick to your stomach." As the stomach contractions get stronger, the vomiting center makes the valve at the top of the stomach pop open, and you throw up. All your stomach's contents go gushing up through the esophagus and out of your mouth. This is actually your body's way of protecting you—by getting rid of the poisons.

The contractions in your small intestine also continue and get stronger. You may feel these contractions as painful cramps, but they are helping to get rid of the poison by moving partially digested food along much faster than usual. You may get a sudden urge to go to the bathroom, and when you do, your stools (body wastes, or excrement) are soft or even liquid. You

SUMMERTIME AND THE LIVING IS QUEASY

Summer is a time for picnics and barbecues with family and friends. What could be nicer than warm weather and good food? Unfortunately, those also happen to be the perfect conditions for microorganisms to multiply. In the hot summer sun, microorganisms can multiply in food really fast, especially when the temperature is above 90°F (32°C). Since more people eat outside during the summer months than any other time of the year, it's no wonder that summertime is peak season for food poisoning.

Eating outside in the summer can be lots of fun. Just be sure not to leave food out in the sun for too long.

have diarrhea. The stools are so watery because the wastes did not spend much time in your large intestine, where excess water is normally removed. Diarrhea is not a pleasant experience, but it removes millions of bacteria from your body.

As more and more body cells are damaged, a buildup of chemicals is being released in the body. Soon inflammation develops in the muscles, and your body aches. In the meantime, the numerous trips to the bathroom have made you lose a serious amount of water, and you become dehydrated. You feel tired, and your head starts to pound.

As the *Salmonella* bacteria continue to spread, the immune system calls for reinforcements. More white blood cells swarm in. Some have grown into giant cells, twice the usual size. They are called macrophages, which literally means "big eaters." That is exactly what they do—they gobble up bacteria and digest them, breaking them down with powerful proteins called enzymes. Meanwhile, other white blood cells have attached bits of *Salmonella* to their outer surface, like warriors that take trophies from defeated enemies. These cells travel through the bloodstream and help the immune system to recognize the enemy bacteria.

In the lymph nodes (bean-shaped clusters of immune system cells), specialized cells turn into antibody-making factories. The huge numbers of antibodies they produce can attach to the chemicals on the outside of *Salmonella* bacteria. Some of these antibodies damage the bacteria; others make them easier for the macrophages to catch and kill. As the body's defenders are strengthened by all these reinforcements, they begin to win their battles against the invading germs. Within a few days, the numbers of bacteria have dropped substantially, and the bouts of nausea and diarrhea stop. Still, it will take a few weeks for the white blood cells to kill all of the *Salmonella* remaining in your body. White blood cell scavengers act as a clean-up squad, gobbling up bacteria and bits of dead body cells. Finally you are back to normal.

After consuming contaminated food, the body starts to fight the invading germs. This may result in cramps, vomiting, or diarrhea.

GERMS ARE OFTEN THE CULPRIT

Most cases of food poisoning are caused by bacteria or viruses. These germs are microorganisms—tiny creatures that cannot be seen without a microscope. Viruses are even smaller than bacteria. They can live only in people and other living things. Diseases such as colds, flu, and chickenpox are caused by viruses. Bacteria are everywhere—on human skin, inside the body, in the air, in food and water, and on everything we touch. Most of them do not cause any harm. In fact, some are even helpful. Bacteria in our intestines, for example, help to digest our food and make vitamins for us. Sometimes, though, even normally harmless microorganisms can make us sick. Under the right conditions—warmth, moisture, and plenty of food—germs can multiply to harmful levels.

RECOGNIZE THE SYMPTOMS

Food poisoning can have a variety of causes, so symptoms can vary. However, many types of food poisoning do share some common symptoms: nausea, vomiting, abdominal cramps, and diarrhea. It takes time after exposure for symptoms to develop. This is called the incubation period. How long it takes depends on the type of organism or toxin that was swallowed, and how much of it survived the acid bath in the stomach. Many people think that food poisoning is caused by the last meal that the sick person ate, but that is not always true. Symptoms may develop in as little as thirty minutes after eating the contaminated food, or they may be delayed for days or even weeks. Often the symptoms get worse as time goes by.

Pregnant women and young children are two of the groups that are at an increased risk of suffering a severe reaction to food poisoning.

Symptoms may develop in as little as thirty minutes after eating the contaminated food, or they may be delayed for days or even weeks.

Health experts say that certain groups of people have a higher risk than others of getting sick from food poisoning, and of having more serious problems. These high-risk groups include:

- the elderly (because their immune system may not be as strong as when they were younger)
- infants and young children (because their immune system is not yet fully developed)
- people with chronic disease (such as diabetes, cancer, or AIDS), whose immune systems are weakened
- pregnant women (food poisoning leads to dehydration and may harm or even kill the unborn child)

Chapter 4

How the Trouble Starts

Growing up in the British town of Wigan, Zoe Jeffries enjoyed entering dance contests and doing gymnastics.[1] At the age of twelve, she was a popular and outgoing girl. But in May 1998, everything started to change. First Zoe complained of leg pains. Then came the headaches. Soon Zoe began behaving differently. Her mother says the change in her daughter was dramatic. "It was as though she went to bed one person and got up a completely different person."[2] Zoe was having crying fits that often lasted for hours at a time. She refused to go to school and would not leave the house. Zoe's mother thought that her daughter was probably reacting to her father's death. (He had died of a heart attack a few months earlier.) Not knowing what else to do, Mrs. Jeffries took Zoe to the doctor.

The doctor thought that Zoe was depressed and prescribed antidepressants for her. The medication did not seem to help, though. In fact, Zoe was getting worse. She was fighting with her friends. Her behavior got so bad that she could no longer go to school. She started to pull at her hair, sometimes yanking

Cows infected with a certain protein are the source of variant Creutzfeldt-Jakob disease, the human form of mad cow disease.

so hard that she wound up with handfuls of it. Then she was having hallucinations about "gremlins" coming into her room at night. The doctors continued to say that she was suffering from depression.

By the end of the year, Zoe was having trouble walking. She was dragging one foot and sometimes lost her balance. By early 1999, Zoe needed a wheelchair to get around. The doctors ran a number of tests, and eventually an MRI diagnosed Zoe's problem—variant Creutzfeldt-Jakob disease, or vCJD. What kind of disease was this and how did Zoe get it? Mrs. Jeffries was given pamphlets and learned that vCJD is related to mad cow disease. Zoe had gotten sick from eating contaminated beef. She had been eating burgers and meat pies since she was two years old, as many as three times a week. After hearing this news, the Jeffries family stopped eating meat altogether.[3] But it was too late for Zoe. She died in 2000 at the age of fourteen.

MICROBIAL CULPRITS

Among the more than 250 known foodborne illnesses, mad cow disease—as many people call it—is a rare and unusual type of food poisoning. Most types of food poisoning are caused by bacteria or other microorganisms. The illnesses caused by some of them are so common that many people are familiar with their names.

Here are some common causes of food poisoning:

Salmonella. *Salmonella* is a kind of bacterium that can cause several illnesses. *Salmonella typhi* causes typhoid fever. Other types of *Salmonella* cause a type of food poisoning called salmonellosis. *Salmonella* poisoning is one of the most common causes of foodborne illness. Every year, about forty thousand cases of *Salmonella* infections are reported in the United States. However, the CDC believes that the actual number could be more than thirty times that amount because many cases are so mild that they go undiagnosed.[4]

Cookie dough might taste good, but it contains raw eggs that when eaten could cause food poisoning.

CAN PETS BE POISONOUS?

Many people like to keep reptiles and amphibians as pets. What they may not realize is that these animals may carry Salmonella, *the bacterium that is typically linked with food poisoning.* Salmonella *can be found in the animal's feces and can spread to people when the pet is handled. Some children, especially, may touch pets and then put their hands in their mouths. People should always wash their hands after handling a reptile or amphibian.*

Salmonella has been found mostly in raw and undercooked eggs, undercooked and raw meat, and milk products. Bacteria from these foods can settle in the small intestine and multiply. They produce a toxin that can damage or kill body cells. When enough cells are harmed (usually within twelve to seventy-two hours after exposure), symptoms start to develop. They may include fever, diarrhea, stomach cramps, nausea, and vomiting. Symptoms usually go away on their own within four to seven days. The illness may become much more serious for people in high-risk groups. In such people the bacteria may spread to other parts of the body and damage important organs, which can result in death. An estimated four hundred people die from salmonellosis in the United States each year.[5]

Salmonella can be killed by high temperatures. That is why it is very important to cook eggs, poultry, and meat completely, to wipe out any *Salmonella* bacteria they may contain. And people should always wash their hands after handling eggs, raw meat, or poultry. Otherwise, the bacteria could get into their body if they touch their eyes, nose, or mouth.

Deli meats may carry the *Listeria* bacterium, so women are advised to avoid lunch meat during pregnancy.

Campylobacter. Although *Salmonella* is the best-known cause of food poisoning, *Campylobacter* is actually the most common cause of foodborne illness. *Campylobacter* is a bacterium that causes an illness called campylobacteriosis. It is estimated that 1.3 million Americans are affected by this germ each year.[6]

Campylobacter has been found in raw or undercooked meat and poultry, unpasteurized milk, untreated drinking water, and raw or undercooked shellfish. Within two to five days after exposure, the infected person may develop diarrhea, cramping, stomach pain, and fever. Diarrhea may become bloody. The illness usually goes away on its own within a week. Some with severe cases may take antimicrobial therapy. However, people in high-risk groups may develop complications, such as Guillain-Barre syndrome, a rare condition that can cause paralysis. Although *Campylobacter* infections do not usually lead to

E. COLI IN SPINACH

In September 2006, grocery stores in more than twenty states had to pull bags of prepackaged spinach off the shelves. The Food and Drug Administration reported that 199 people had diarrhea and dehydration from eating the spinach. Three people died and thirty-one had kidney failure. The illnesses and deaths were all caused by E. coli *O157:H7 infections. Health officials believe that the spinach could have become contaminated either in the field or during packaging. The bacteria may also have gotten into the water used to irrigate the crops. Wild pigs that had broken through the fences around the spinach field may have carried in the bacteria. The pigs tested positive for the same* E. coli *strain that caused the outbreak. Dole recalled all bagged spinach from shelves across the country. This was the twentieth outbreak of food poisoning linked to fresh spinach or lettuce since 1995.*[7]

death, the CDC estimates that seventy-six Americans die from this illness each year.[8]

Listeria. *Listeria* is a bacterium that causes an infection called listeriosis. This illness has recently been discovered to be a serious health problem in the United States. It affects mainly pregnant women, newborns, and adults with weakened immune systems. While it may not be as well-known as some other foodborne illnesses, listeriosis is much more deadly. The CDC estimates about 1,600 people are infected by *Listeria* in the United States each year. Of these people, 260 die.[9]

Listeria is commonly found in plants, animals, water, and soil. The bacteria can be spread to people through untreated water, unpasteurized milk and dairy products, raw meat and seafood, and fruits and vegetables grown in contaminated soil or fertilized with infected manure. *Listeria* can be killed by high temperatures, but some ready-to-eat foods, such as cold cuts, may become contaminated during packaging, after they have already been cooked.

When *Listeria* invade the human body, it may take two to thirty days for symptoms to develop. Adults infected with *Listeria* may develop a fever, chills, nausea, and diarrhea. An infant may throw up, refuse to drink, or have trouble breathing. Serious complications may occur, such as blood poisoning or meningitis (inflammation of the coverings of the brain). The infection may be fatal to a pregnant woman's unborn child. These complications can be avoided if the illness is caught early enough and treated with medicine.

***E. coli* O157:H7.** While hundreds of strains of *E. coli* bacteria exist, most are harmless. But this particular strain—*E. coli* O157:H7—is damaging. (The O157:H7 part of the name allows scientists to distinguish it from other strains.) Shiga toxin-producing *E. coli* (STEC), also called Verocytotoxin-producing *E. coli* (VTEC) or enterohemorrhagic *E. coli* (EHEC), is the one most commonly heard about in the news in association with

A 2006 outbreak of *E. coli* forced supermarkets across the country to remove bagged spinach from their shelves.

foodborne outbreaks. It produces a powerful toxin that can make people extremely sick. An estimated 265,000 STEC infections occur each year in the United States. STEC O157 causes about 36 percent of these infections.[10] About sixty-one people die from the infection each year.[11]

E. coli O157:H7 has been found in raw or undercooked ground beef, salami, unpasteurized milk and juice, sprouts, salad greens, and untreated water. People can also become infected by swimming in water contaminated with animal or human waste. Within three to four days after exposure, the infected person may develop severe stomach cramps, followed by diarrhea that often turns bloody. Other symptoms may include nausea, vomiting, and a low-grade fever. In most cases, the illness goes away on its own in five to ten days. In high-risk groups, especially in children under five and the elderly, the illness can lead to hemolytic uremic syndrome (HUS), a condition that can result in kidney failure. This complication occurs in about 2 to 7 percent of *E. coli* infections.[12]

Shigella. *Shigella* is a kind of bacterium that causes an illness called shigellosis. About fourteen thousand cases are reported in the United States every year. However, the actual number may be twenty times that amount because milder cases usually are not diagnosed or reported. Children, especially two- to four-year-olds, are most likely to get this disease.[13] *Shigella* is typically spread by people who do not wash their hands after going to the bathroom and then serve food to others. (Like many other foodborne bacteria, *Shigella* is found in the feces of infected people.) Outbreaks often occur in crowded places, such as day-care centers and nursing homes. Shigellosis is much more common in developing countries, where conditions are often crowded and not particularly clean.

Shigella has been found in raw or undercooked poultry, unpasteurized milk and dairy products, and salad greens. If a person does become infected, symptoms will start to develop within a day or two after eating the contaminated food. Symptoms may include stomach cramps, fever, and diarrhea, which often turns bloody. The illness goes away on its own within five to seven days. For some people, especially young children and the elderly, severe diarrhea may lead to dehydration and a trip to the hospital may be necessary.

Botulism. Botulism is a rare but deadly illness. It is caused by a powerful toxin produced by the bacterium *Clostridium botulinum*. There are actually three main kinds of botulism: foodborne, infant, and wound. Foodborne botulism accounts for only 15 percent of the estimated 145 cases of botulism reported in the United States each year. Infant botulism makes up the majority—about 65 percent—of the reported cases. The remaining cases are wound botulism. In the past half century,

If people do not wash their hands after using the bathroom, they risk spreading germs to those around them.

the proportion of patients with botulism who die has dropped from about 50 percent to less than 5 percent.[14]

Botulinum bacteria are commonly found in soil and dust. Wound botulism occurs when the bacteria enter a cut or wound and then release their poison into the body.

Infant botulism may develop when babies put dirty items containing botulinum bacteria into their mouths. The bacteria get into their bodies, multiply in their intestines, and release their toxin. Some cases of infant botulism are actually a type of foodborne illness. They are caused by eating honey, which sometimes contains botulinum bacteria. Researchers suggest that the bees that make the honey may have picked up the bacteria from the environment. (Health experts advise that honey should not be given to babies under one year old.)

Foodborne botulism is often caused by eating foods that have been canned or preserved at home. The bacteria may have been picked up from the soil in which the fruit or vegetables were grown, or they were introduced during handling. Ordinary boiling will kill most germs, but botulinum bacteria can survive by changing into a special form, called a spore. Bacterial spores are covered by a thick, tough overcoat and just rest until conditions are better for growth. Usually the combination of high temperature and high pressure during the canning process *does* kill botulinum bacteria.

Botulism from commercial canned foods is extremely rare. In home canning, however, the temperature and pressure may not be high enough to kill all the spores. The few spores that survive become active again in the sealed canned foods, multiplying and producing their toxin. Botulinum bacteria are most likely to grow in foods with a low acid level, such as asparagus, green beans, beets, and corn. (Tomatoes and pickles

A PRETTY POISON?

Botulinum toxin is one of the deadliest of all poisons, but doctors have found a use for it. They use this toxin, in a purified form called BOTOX, to safely treat various muscle problems, such as constant twitching in an eyelid, arm, or leg. Injecting a tiny amount of BOTOX blocks the incoming messages from the nerves to the muscles and stops the twitching. When injected into the muscles of the face, BOTOX can smooth out wrinkles—but the effects last only a few months, and then another injection is needed. More and more people are using BOTOX to get rid of their wrinkles so that they can stay young-looking. BOTOX has also been approved as a treatment for excessive sweating.

are usually too acidic for the bacteria to grow.) To be safe, home-canned foods should be boiled for at least ten minutes before eating. This will destroy toxins produced by any bacteria that survived.

When a person eats food contaminated with the botulinum bacteria, it may take eighteen to thirty-six hours for symptoms to develop. (Symptoms can develop in as soon as six hours, however, or as late as ten days.) Botulinum toxin targets the nervous system, which can lead to serious problems. Symptoms may include blurred or double vision, muscle weakness, slurred speech, droopy eyelids, and difficulty swallowing. If the illness is not treated, it can lead to paralysis in the arms, legs, trunk, and even breathing muscles. When the breathing muscles are affected, botulism may result in death. Protect yourself by throwing out any bulging or swollen cans in your home. Bulging, which may be a sign of contamination, is due to a buildup of gas produced by the growing bacteria.

Noroviruses. The germs most commonly involved in food poisoning are noroviruses (also called Norwalk-like viruses). Chances are that people who say they have the "stomach flu" are probably infected with these viruses. The CDC estimates that noroviruses cause about nineteen to twenty-one million cases of acute gastroenteritis (inflammation of the stomach or intestines or both).[15] Like many food-poisoning bacteria, noroviruses are found in the vomit and stool of infected people. The viruses can spread very easily in a number of ways: by consuming food or drink contaminated with the norovirus; by touching contaminated objects, such as a doorknob, and then touching one's mouth; or through direct contact with the infected person or sharing his or her food or utensils.

Noroviruses can spread very quickly in crowded places, such as day-care centers, nursing homes, and cruise ships. Symptoms start to develop within twenty-four to forty-eight hours after exposure. They may include a lot of vomiting,

Home-canned goods pose a risk of foodborne illness. The canned foods found in supermarkets, however, are generally very safe.

diarrhea along with stomach cramps, and nausea. Some people may also develop a low-grade fever, chills, headache, muscle aches, and a general feeling of tiredness.

Although noroviruses can make a person really miserable, most people feel better within one to two days. However, people in high-risk groups may become seriously dehydrated and should seek medical attention. Antibiotics do not work with the norovirus infection because it is a viral (not a bacterial) infection.

Mad cow disease. Although this foodborne illness had been in the headlines a lot in the 1990s and early 2000s, mad cow disease is actually very rare. It is caused by defective proteins, called prions, which are found in the brain tissue of infected cattle. Prions literally eat away at the brain, leaving spongelike holes. It can take as long as ten years for symptoms to develop. The cow becomes aggressive and has trouble walking. Eventually, it dies.

If people eat meat from infected cattle, they may develop the human form of mad cow disease, known as variant Creutzfeldt-Jakob disease (vCJD). Signs and symptoms of vCJD may include memory loss, mood changes, dizziness, difficulty walking, muscle spasms, loss of speech, and blindness.

No way to kill prions has yet been discovered. Prions survive in conditions that would kill most bacteria and viruses, including extreme heat, ultraviolet light and other radiation, and disinfectants. Animals and people infected with prions are likely to die.

Mad cow disease first appeared in dairy cows in Great Britain in the mid-1980s. Thousands of cows were affected. The disease spread rapidly through infected feed. Farmers commonly included animal parts in cattle feed to provide extra protein for growing. Some of these parts were infected with prions. News of this "mad cow disease" stirred up panic in people all over Britain.

Noroviruses can spread quickly through a crowded day-care center.

The first human case of infection with the prions of mad cow disease was diagnosed in 1994. As more human cases were reported, various countries took legal action to prevent it from spreading. Starting in March 1996, British beef could no longer be exported to other countries. In 1997 the use of animal parts in cattle feed was officially banned. Even though the source was eliminated, many cattle were already infected and would not show symptoms for many years. In 2000 health officials required testing for prions throughout Europe in efforts to keep the infected cattle out of the food supply. In 2009 the US Food and Drug Administration (FDA) established enhanced mad cow-related feed bans to help prevent the disease.

By April 2005 more than 184,000 cases of mad cow disease had occurred in cattle in Great Britain alone.[16] The risk of infecting humans is very low, however. By 2005 there was a total of about 225 cases of mad cow disease in cows and that number dropped to eleven in 2010. Many Americans worried about mad cow disease and the safety of the beef in the United States. However, only twenty-four cases in cattle have ever been identified in North America as of February 2015, according to the CDC. Still, on April 24, 2012, one cow in California tested positive for the disease, so health officials and cattle farmers remain vigilant.[17]

FOODS THAT ARE ALREADY POISONOUS

Some foods contain their own natural poisons and may be harmful if you eat them. Certain fungi, for example, contain poisons that can make people sick. Mushrooms, molds, mildew, and yeast are all fungi. Actually thousands of different kinds of mushrooms grow in North America, but only about a hundred of them are poisonous. The mushrooms sold in stores are not harmful, and many people love to eat them. Just be sure not to pick any wild mushrooms unless you are an expert. It is

Front pages of newspapers in 1996 demonstrate the outrage resulting from mad cow disease.

not easy to identify whether a mushroom is poisonous or not, so it is usually best to leave them alone.

You may have seen that gray, fuzzy-looking stuff that grows on foods left in the refrigerator too long. That's mold, and like mushrooms, it is a type of fungus. If you look at mold under a microscope, it will look like skinny mushrooms. Mold forms spores, which can float through the air and land on food, where they can grow and reproduce if the conditions are right. Mold grows best in warm and moist conditions. But unlike most bacteria, mold and other fungi can live in very hot or very cold environments. That is why refrigerating food may keep bacteria from growing, but it won't keep mold from growing on fruits and vegetables, or in a jar of spaghetti sauce. Cooking moldy food at high temperatures will not kill the mold spores.

You might get sick from eating a slice of moldy bread or a piece of moldy cheese, but these kinds of molds usually do not cause serious harm. Some molds, however, produce poisonous substances called mycotoxins. These molds are found mainly in grains and nuts, although they may also grow on celery, grape juice, apples, and other produce. Probably the best known and most carefully studied mycotoxin is aflatoxin. This is a cancer-causing poison found in certain molds that grow mainly in stored crops, especially peanuts and corn. Aflatoxin has been linked to a number of diseases in livestock, domestic animals, and humans all over the world.

Clams, oysters, and other shellfish may become contaminated with poisons from the water creatures on which they feed. Much of their diet includes algae and other microscopic organisms (called plankton) that live in the surface waters. At certain times of the year, some of the plankton organisms, such as red algae, have a sudden population explosion, multiplying in such huge numbers that they stain the water red. (These times are known as red tides.) Plankton can produce poisonous

Do not eat mushrooms found in the wild unless you are absolutely certain they are safe. Some kinds of mushrooms can be poisonous.

chemicals that become concentrated in the bodies of animals that feed on them, especially during red tides.

Oysters in the Gulf of Mexico have been known to get infected with *Vibrio vulnificus*, a bacterium commonly found in those waters. It's the same bacterium that causes cholera. Between 1998 and 2007, the CDC recorded nine hundred cases of poisoning by this bacterium in Gulf Coast states. The condition can be serious and require antibiotics.[18]

These days, shellfish is monitored and tested regularly, so the risk of eating this kind of contaminated shellfish is very low. However, eating raw shellfish can be risky because they may carry disease-causing viruses and parasites. They may pick up hepatitis A virus, for example, if the waters in which they grow are contaminated by sewage.

Most fruits and vegetables are sprayed with pesticides, chemicals that farmers use to get rid of insects and other pests. Fruits and vegetables should be washed before eating them so that these chemicals won't get into your body. Eating just one

IS NO ONE SAFE?

At the Food Safety Summit in April 2014 in Baltimore, more than 1,500 attendees came from forty-two states, Canada, Mauritius, and Costa Rica. They all were there to discuss ways to prevent food poisoning. After lunch was served on April 9, about 216 of the participants took ill with diarrhea and some vomiting. It turns out that all those who had gotten sick had eaten the chicken marsala. Since the conference was basically filled with food detectives, they were able to identify the mostly likely culprit as Clostridium perfringens. *This bacterium is commonly found in raw meat and poultry. It just goes to show you that food poisoning can affect anyone.*[19]

Shellfish can be contaminated by organisms found in the water.

apple without washing it will not harm you. It will probably contain only traces of pesticides. However, if you never wash the foods you eat, poisons may build up in your body. It may take years, but eventually they could damage important organs, like the brain, heart, and liver.

The Environmental Protection Agency (EPA) sets limits for the amounts of pesticides and other chemicals that may remain in foods. These "residues" are so small that they are not considered harmful. The FDA and the US Department of Agriculture (USDA) check foods to make sure that they do not contain residues above the legal limits. State agencies also test foods produced locally. Moreover, chemical companies are developing pesticides that are less toxic to humans.

Chapter 5

Spotting the Problem and Taking Action

For years, Carole Sugarman has worked as a food writer for *The Washington Post* and *Bethesda* magazine. She has written numerous articles about foodborne illnesses and food safety. She has plenty of experience in interviewing victims of foodborne illnesses and parents whose children have died from them. Although she knew a lot about food poisoning from others she didn't know much about it firsthand. But then Carole's nine-year-old daughter, Anna, developed a bad case of *Salmonella* poisoning after eating one of her favorite chicken meals from a restaurant. Carole strongly suspected that the chicken was undercooked.

After eating her favorite bird, Anna suddenly developed severe stomach pains and bouts of diarrhea that sent her dashing to the bathroom. Feeling absolutely miserable, she told her mom it was like "having my butt on full blast."[1] When Anna became weaker and dehydrated, her parents took her to the hospital.

After hearing about Anna's symptoms, a doctor in the emergency room suspected appendicitis and ordered a battery of tests, including a sonogram, an X-ray, and a CT scan. Carole, however, believed that her daughter might have a foodborne illness. She suggested that the doctor take a stool culture, which is the standard diagnostic test for foodborne illness. The doctor ignored her request. Patricia was annoyed. She agreed that it was a good idea to rule out appendicitis, but food poisoning seemed like another obvious possibility.

Another doctor came on duty that night, and Carole asked her to take a stool sample. The doctor agreed, although she thought Anna probably had a gastrointestinal virus—like five other kids who had been treated in the ER that night. When the test results finally came back a few days later, they showed that Anna had salmonellosis.

Anna recalled that some of the chicken tenders had been cold and hard. Carole's hunch was right. She later asked an ER doctor why they don't take stool cultures anymore. She was told that the results are not very helpful since they usually do not come back for a couple of days. In the case of food poisoning, a positive test result does not have any effect on the treatment. (In fact, for many cases there is no specific treatment except to keep the patient hydrated.) Doctors generally focus on treating their individual patients. What is the point of running tests that will not help the patients get well?

Carole saw things differently. She knew how important it was to identify foodborne illnesses. By doing so, health agencies could keep track of outbreaks and protect people from future contaminations.

In the meantime, Anna was prescribed the typical treatment for food poisoning: the BRAT diet. *BRAT* stands for *b*ananas, *r*ice, *a*pplesauce, and *t*oast, which are foods that are easy on the stomach and help the digestive system get back to normal. After two weeks of missing school, Anna was feeling

Eating at a restaurant should be an enjoyable and safe experience. Be specific about how you want your meal prepared, and if it does not look fully cooked, send the food back.

like her old self again. The experience has not made her nervous about eating out at restaurants, but she and her mother are careful to order meats that are fully cooked. And she also started ordering grilled cheese instead of chicken.[2]

HOW TO KNOW FOR SURE

Every year, millions of people get food poisoning, but most of them do not go to the doctor. Usually they feel better within a day or two, so these cases go unreported. Many people do not even realize that the illness they have is food poisoning. The symptoms are often confused with those of a common viral infection. In fact, people who describe symptoms of nausea, vomiting, or diarrhea tend to say that they have the "stomach flu" or a "stomach virus."

Many medical experts do not like the term stomach flu because they believe it causes confusion about what flu (influenza) really is. The influenza virus targets the respiratory system—the breathing passages and lungs. The viruses that attack the gastrointestinal system—the stomach and intestines—are quite different. They cause vomiting and diarrhea, which are not symptoms of the flu.

Every year, millions of people get food poisoning, but most of them do not go to the doctor. Usually they feel better within a day or two, so these cases go unreported.

Diagnosing food poisoning can take some detective work. The doctor must ask some key questions that will give clues to

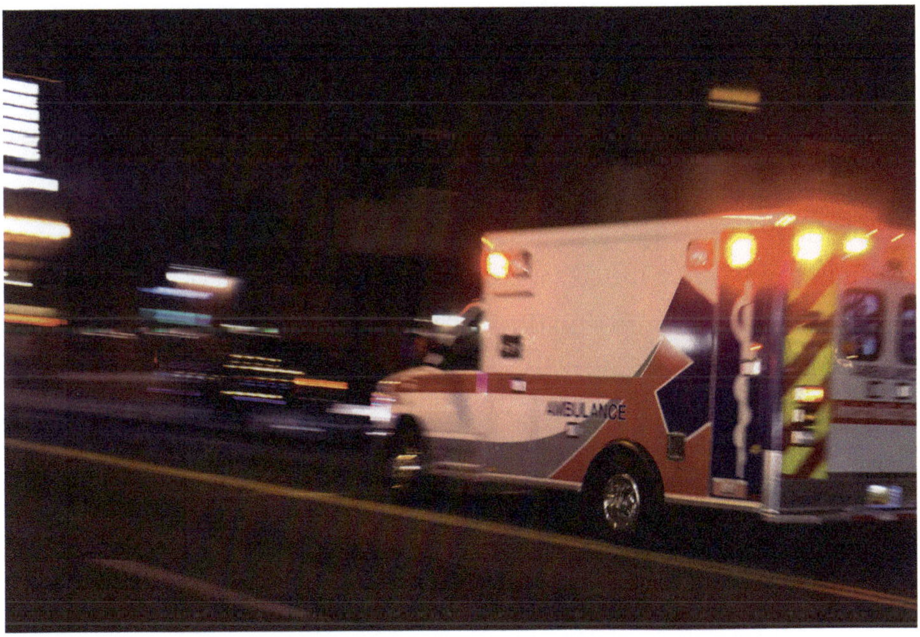

When foodborne illness results in severe symptoms, it is important to get the ill person to a hospital.

Your doctor will ask questions and perform tests to determine if you are suffering from a foodborne illness.

the patient's illness: What are your symptoms? When did you first get sick? What have you eaten in the last few days? Did you eat the meals at home or at a restaurant? Has anyone else in your family gotten sick? After gathering all the clues, the doctor may make an initial diagnosis of food poisoning. Tests can confirm the diagnosis. However, treatment is usually started right away, since it takes a couple of days for the test results to come back—and treatment is basically the same in most cases. Early treatment is especially important for botulism, which can have devastating effects on the patient and can lead to death if left untreated.

A stool culture is the standard diagnostic test for food poisoning. The patient provides a stool sample, which is then cultured—grown in a laboratory under conditions that allow bacteria to multiply. When enough bacteria have grown, the technician can identify the type of organisms that are causing the illness. Other diagnostic tests can be performed to isolate the bacteria from vomit, blood, or any leftover contaminated

COULD IT BE ALLERGY?

What might look like food poisoning could actually be an allergy. Many people have problems when they eat certain foods because they are allergic to them. An allergy causes a person's body to overreact to a substance that does not normally bother most people. If someone has an allergy to strawberries, for example, eating a couple of them may give this person a bad stomachache or produce a skin rash. Allergies to peanuts may cause breathing difficulty and other serious—even life-threatening—reactions.

Some people can't drink milk or eat other dairy products. Their bodies have a problem digesting these foods properly. These people have a condition called lactose intolerance. Milk contains lactose, which is a milk sugar. People with lactose intolerance don't have an enzyme called lactase, which is needed to digest milk products. When they drink milk or eat cheese or ice cream, they may get a stomachache, gas, or diarrhea.

food. In some very rare cases, doctors may do further testing on patients whose symptoms do not seem to be going away. For example, a sigmoidoscopy is a test that involves a long, thin, hollow tube used to look at the inside of a patient's large intestine to find the source of bleeding or infection.

GETTING THE RIGHT TREATMENT

When it comes to the treatment of food poisoning, there is one main focus: to replace the fluids and electrolytes lost through vomiting and diarrhea. Electrolytes are salts and minerals that the body needs to stay healthy. A loss of fluids can lead to dehydration. Your body is two-thirds water, so when you become dehydrated, the body cannot function properly. Patients should drink plenty of fluids, especially those that help replace electrolytes. Coconut water is a good source of potassium, sodium, and magnesium, and it also offers fiber. Pedialyte® is a beverage packed with electrolytes. Sports drinks, such as Gatorade® brand, are not as effective in replacing these lost electrolytes, and are not usually recommended as treatment for diarrheal illness. Taking antidiarrheal medicines, such as Pepto-Bismol® tablets or liquid, can help prevent dehydration.

During times of vomiting and diarrhea, people with food poisoning should try not to eat any solid food. They do need to keep hydrated, though, by drinking small amounts of clear liquids, such as water or ginger ale, throughout the day. Once vomiting and diarrhea have stopped, health experts recommend the BRAT diet for two to three days. Certain foods should be avoided at least for the first few days. They include milk and other dairy products, spicy foods, greasy fried foods, and raw fruits and vegetables high in insoluble fiber.

Doctors do not usually prescribe antibiotics to treat food poisoning. Antibiotics are medicines that kill bacteria. They do not work for illnesses caused by viruses. Some severe cases of

It is crucial for someone suffering from food poisoning to stay hydrated.

KNOW WHEN TO GO TO THE DOCTOR

Most cases of food poisoning are not serious, and symptoms often go away on their own. However, some people, especially those in high-risk groups, may develop more serious problems that need immediate medical attention. People should seek medical help if they have any of the following symptoms:

- *High fever (temperature over 101.5°F, or 38.6°C)*
- *Blood in stools or vomit*
- *Severe stomach pains*
- *Signs of dehydration, such as dry mouth, decreased urine, sunken eyes, dizziness*
- *Diarrhea that lasts more than three days (which can lead to dehydration)*
- *Ongoing vomiting that prevents keeping liquids down (which can lead to dehydration)*

bacterial food poisoning can be treated with antibiotics. But these drugs are not usually given to people with mild cases. Medical experts worry that antibiotics are used too often. When bacteria are exposed to an antibiotic, most of them are killed, but some may survive and multiply. These drug-resistant bacteria, which can't be killed by the usual doses of the antibiotic, may be passed on to other people. The more an antibiotic is used, the more likely that drug-resistant bacteria will appear and spread. Then even very high doses of the antibiotic will not work against the disease. The bacteria may become resistant to other drugs, as well.

Botulism is treated differently from other types of bacterial food poisoning. Patients are given an antitoxin, a substance that stops the toxin (released by the bacteria) from causing further damage. The antitoxin should be given soon after symptoms first appear, while most of the toxin is circulating in the body and before it bonds to nerve endings. The doctor may also try to remove any remaining contaminated food that is still in the body by giving the patient either a substance that causes vomiting or an enema that works to loosen stools, forcing the person to go to the bathroom. Patients whose breathing muscles have already been damaged may need support from ventilators (breathing machines).

6 Chapter

When Good Food Goes Bad

Like at many workplaces, the employees at one AT&T building in San Jose shared a refrigerator. The workers all enjoyed having a place to store their food, but with about fifty people sharing the fridge, food was often forgotten and no one wanted to throw out someone else's food.

Gradually, the fridge was building its own rotten environment. Mysterious items that were formerly edible were growing fur. Meats were decomposing. In time, the aroma grew so bad that one employee took action. In May of 2009, she took all the decaying spoiled food out of the fridge to a conference room and cleaned the refrigerator with a strong disinfectant. This employee had recently undergone nasal surgery and didn't smell anything bad. Another worker, however, inhaled the stench, and sprayed a different chemical cleaner in the air to improve matters.

The combination of decomposing foods and cleaners proved to be too much for anyone in the building. All 325 employees were evacuated to the parking lot. The business contacted San Jose's hazmat team to come and help. All told, fifty

If you are unsure whether food is safe to eat, throw it out.

firefighters and eighteen emergency vehicles rushed to the scene. Paramedics checked over those who were overwhelmed by the fumes. One firefighter compared the smell to a rotting dead dog. Ultimately, the offending foods were removed and order was restored to the business. All employees survived except for the haunting memories of horrible food odors.[1]

While most people don't require a hazmat team to help them clean the fridge, many know what it's like to keep items well beyond the point of being edible. Many people keep left-overs in the refrigerator, hoping to eat them in the next day or two. Too often, though, these leftovers are forgotten. They may get pushed to the back of the refrigerator and spend the next several months, or even years, there! When food sits too long, even in the refrigerator, it will go bad. Sometimes the food doesn't look or smell bad, but that doesn't mean that it is good to eat. If you can't remember when you last ate it, it is a good idea to throw it out.

Anyone can become a victim of food poisoning, but you can do many things to reduce your risk. In this chapter, we will discuss some very important rules of food safety that will help you avoid getting sick from the food you eat.

ORGANIC MAY NOT BE SAFER

Foods labeled "organic" have been grown without the use of synthetic pesticides, herbicides, or fertilizers. Some people believe that these foods are worth the higher prices they cost because they do not contain added chemicals that might be toxic. While avoiding these poisons might be a good idea, organic foods can still contain bacteria or disease-causing microbes. The cattle manure that organic farmers use as fertilizer can be a source of E. coli *and other intestinal bacteria. Moreover, organic foods are just as likely as those grown the conventional way to become contaminated with bacteria or viruses during picking, packing, and preparation.*

Always check expiration dates when buying fresh food.

SHOP RIGHT

The first step to keeping your food safe starts in the grocery store. To keep foods fresh, refrigerated items, such as meats, dairy, eggs, and fish, should be the last items put into the shopping cart. Do not buy canned foods that are bulging or dented, or jars that are cracked or have loose or bulging lids. Eggs should also be checked to make sure that they are not cracked. Do not buy unpasteurized milk products, ciders, or juices. Be careful not to buy fruit with bruised or broken skin. Bacteria can enter openings in the skin and contaminate the fruit.

When you are buying meat, poultry, fish, or dairy products, check the label. It should have an "expiration" or "sell by" or "best if used by" date. If the current date is past the date on the label, don't buy the food. Even if the expiration date is still in the future, do not buy anything that smells bad or looks strange.

Packages of meat, fish, or poultry often leak juices. When grocery bags are being packed, bag these items separately from lettuce or other foods that will not be cooked before eating. Do not place bags with meat, poultry, or fish on top of foods or paper products. And watch for leaks when placing foods in the refrigerator. Wipe up any spills with paper towels and disinfectant solution.

KEEP IT COOL

In the grocery store, refrigerated items are the last items to buy. At home, they should be the first items put away—in the refrigerator or freezer. Remember, bacteria multiply in warmer temperatures. Perishable foods—foods that spoil—should never be left out at room temperature for more than two hours. Keeping these foods in the refrigerator or freezer can help to stop bacteria from growing.

Health experts say that a thermostat should be used to make sure the temperatures are cool enough: The refrigerator

Do not overcrowd the refrigerator with food. It will not stay cold enough if air cannot circulate.

should be set to 40°F (about 4°C) or below, and the freezer should be set to 0°F (–18°C). Refrigerators should never be overcrowded with food. Air needs to circulate to keep the food chilled. Freezers, on the other hand, hold their cold best when they are mostly filled with frozen foods. However, the air vents in the freezer should not be blocked.

Raw meat, poultry, and fish should be put in the freezer right away, unless these foods are going to be cooked within the next two days. Wash these items (except for ground meat) before wrapping them for freezing. They should be wrapped in heavy-duty plastic wrap, freezer paper, or aluminum foil and sealed tightly so that they will last longer in the freezer.

Food should never be thawed at room temperature. The surface of the food will thaw long before the center, allowing time for bacteria to multiply. Food can be thawed in the refrigerator overnight. For a quicker thaw, place the food under cold running water, or defrost it in the microwave.

COOK COMPLETELY

Cooking food thoroughly to the proper internal temperature can kill harmful bacteria that cause foodborne illnesses. The internal temperature is the temperature of the food, not that of the oven. A meat thermometer should be used to make sure food is being cooked to the right temperature. Beef roasts and steaks should be cooked to at least 145°F (63°C), ground beef to 160°F (71°C), and poultry to 180°F (82°C). Be sure to wash the meat thermometer after using it to avoid spreading germs from one food to another.

Do you like your steak or roast beef rare or well done? Rare meats are pink in the center, which means that the center part is not completely cooked. Are they safe to eat? Actually, they are, because contamination most often occurs on the surface of a piece of beef. The surface of rare steaks or roasts is cooked thoroughly, and so any bacteria on them have been killed.

WHY STUFFING TAKES EXTRA CARE

What would a Thanksgiving dinner be without a juicy roast turkey, brown and crispy on the outside and stuffed with a mixture of bread, eggs, celery, and spices? If the turkey is not cooked long enough, though, it can lead to a stomachache that is not just due to overeating. The inside of the turkey, where the stuffing was packed, may have been contaminated, and the raw eggs might have contributed bacteria, too. If the temperature inside did not get high enough while the turkey was cooking, bacteria might have remained in the stuffing. While the turkey was sitting at room temperature, bacteria in the stuffing might have multiplied. A meat thermometer can help determine when the stuffing is safely cooked. The little pop-up thermometer that comes in the turkey just tells you when the meat is hot enough—it does not check the stuffing. The temperature of the stuffing should be measured separately, to be sure it has been cooked to 180°F (82°C).

(When grilling steaks or chops on a barbecue, use tongs to handle them. Poking a fork or knife into a raw steak could push surface bacteria into the center.) Rare hamburgers are not safe to eat, however. During grinding, the surface of the pieces of meat is mixed with the center parts. Therefore, any pink parts in the center of a burger may contain live bacteria that could make you sick.

Raw fish and shellfish can be contaminated during handling, and they may also carry bacteria and parasites picked up from the environment. Eating sushi (which is made from pieces of raw fish) can be risky. Marinating the fish with spices and lime juice does not kill the bacteria or parasites. Cooking will make fish safe to eat, but it must be cooked thoroughly. Well-cooked fish loses its shiny appearance and breaks up easily into flakes when poked with a fork.

A microwave oven does not get hot while it is working, but it heats up food very quickly. However, there may be "cold spots" in the food, where bacteria can survive. To thoroughly

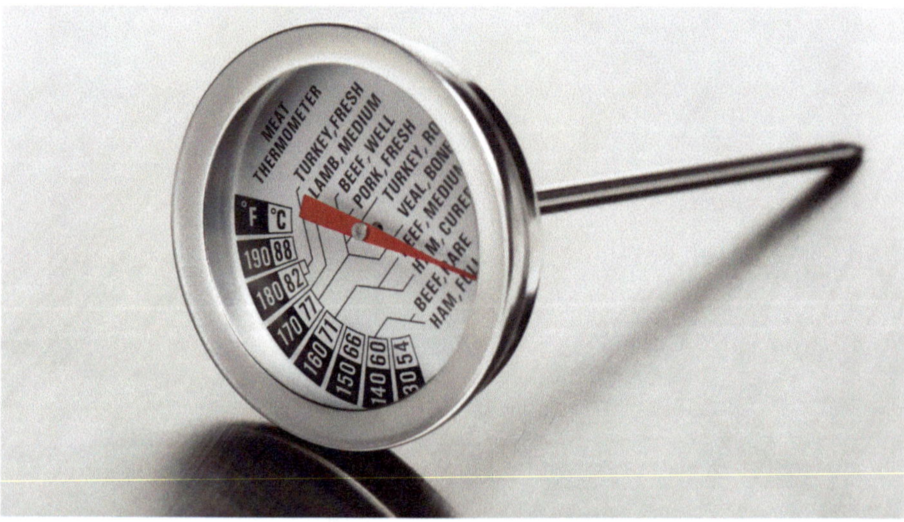

Always use a meat thermometer to ensure the interior of the meat is cooked to the proper temperature.

kill bacteria, turn the dish and stir the contents occasionally so that the food is cooked evenly. Microwave ovens sold today usually have a turntable that rotates the food automatically while it is heating or cooking.

Eggs should be cooked until the yolks and whites are firm, not runny. (Remember, eggs may carry *Salmonella* bacteria.) Do not eat foods that contain raw eggs, such as cookie dough and eggnog. Sauces, soups, and gravies should be heated to a boil. Leftovers should be reheated thoroughly to at least 165°F (74°C).

KEEP IT CLEAN; KEEP IT HEALTHY

If you walk into a restaurant bathroom, you will probably notice a sign reminding workers to wash their hands. This rule is very important, especially for cooks and servers, who could easily spread their germs to other people's food. Washing hands with warm, soapy water will get rid of harmful bacteria that might be on them. But hands need to be washed for more than a couple of seconds. Health experts say that to send the bacteria down the drain you should wash your hands for at least twenty seconds.

Washing hands is a good rule to follow at home, as well. People should always wash their hands after playing with pets, changing diapers, and, of course, going to the bathroom. Germs can spread easily, especially in a kitchen. Bacteria can spread to your hands, countertops, utensils, cutting boards, and then to other foods, making them more likely to cause illness. Health experts call this cross-contamination. It is important to wash hands, utensils, and surfaces thoroughly before and after handling food.

Fruits and vegetables that will be eaten raw should first be washed. Even oranges, melons, and other fruits whose outer covering is not eaten need to be washed, because a knife or

Clean everything thoroughly after preparing a meal, including dishes, utensils, and all surfaces.

fingers might carry bacteria from the surface into the fruit during preparation.

Do not use the same cutting board for raw vegetables that was used for raw meats. Germs can spread from one food to another when raw meat is first cut on a cutting board and then the unwashed cutting board is used to chop raw vegetables. If possible, use two separate cutting boards, one for meats and one for vegetables. Always wash cutting boards thoroughly with soap and hot water between uses.

Use a paper towel to clean up meat juices, and then throw the towel away. This is a better choice than a sponge that is often used to wipe the kitchen sink and counters. Lots of germs can grow on a kitchen sponge; it is damp and contains bits of food on which bacteria can feed. To keep a sponge from getting smelly, wash it thoroughly with a disinfectant solution that kills bacteria and fungi. Once it gets smelly, throw it out. A dishcloth may be used to clean countertops, but it can get just as dirty as a sponge. Dishcloths should be hung to dry between uses, and they should be washed frequently in the washing machine.

Always wash cutting boards thoroughly in hot water between uses. Use a paper towel to clean up meat juices, and then throw the towel away.

Is your refrigerator packed with food? Chances are some of that food has been in there for too long. Experts say that people should clean out their refrigerators once a week. If the milk smells a little funny, or you notice mold growing on the left-overs, don't try it to see if it tastes okay. (You will not get food poisoning from eating a moldy piece of cheese, but it probably won't taste very good. You may be able to save some of the cheese by cutting off the moldy part. Cheese is one of the few foods for which this practice is safe.) Even if food looks and smells okay, it may not be safe to eat. If it is past its expiration date, throw it out. The same is true for a container of leftovers that has been in there for over four or five days. When it comes to cleaning out the refrigerator, just remember: When in doubt, throw it out!

IRRADIATION TO KILL BACTERIA

The idea of irradiated food scares a lot of people. When they hear the word radiation, they think of cancer and other harmful effects. Actually, though, radiation is all around us. A microwave oven uses radiation to cook foods. If you break your arm, the doctor can use an X-ray machine to send radiation through your arm to take a picture of the bones inside. The air is filled with radio waves that radios and TV sets can turn into sounds and pictures. Even sunshine contains radiation—not only light but also heat and ultraviolet (UV) rays.

Radiation is energy carried in the form of rays or tiny particles too small to see without a very powerful microscope. Most of the radiation in our world is present in small amounts or does not contain enough energy to do any harm. Many repeated exposures to radiation can be dangerous, though: too much sun or having too many X-rays, for example.

When foods are irradiated, they are treated with high-energy gamma rays, X-rays, or electrons. The radiation kills bacteria and other microorganisms. Irradiation can also help to control insects and parasites and prevent spoilage. After the treatment, no radiation remains in the food. Therefore, eating irradiated food will not expose you to "harmful radiation." Irradiation may change some of the food chemicals, however, resulting in changes in taste and a loss of small amounts of nutrients. (Cooking foods also changes their taste and destroys some of the nutrients.)

The FDA and the USDA have approved the use of irradiation for a variety of foods, including spices, fruits, vegetables,

THE FUNDAMENTAL FOUR

Remember these four basic rules of food safety:

- ***Clean.*** *Wash hands, utensils, and surfaces before and after handling food, and always wash hands after going to the bathroom. Wash fruits and vegetables thoroughly to remove pesticides, dirt, and bacteria before eating.*
- ***Separate.*** *Avoid cross-contamination by keeping raw meats, poultry, and seafood separate from salads and other ready-to-eat foods.*
- ***Cook.*** *Cook meats, poultry, fish, and eggs thoroughly. Use a meat thermometer to check the internal temperature of the foods.*
- ***Chill.*** *Refrigerate or freeze perishables, prepared foods, and leftovers within two hours. Do not thaw food at room temperature. Instead, use the refrigerator, cold running water, or a microwave oven. Do not crowd the refrigerator with food. Air needs to circulate to cool food properly.*

raw meats, and poultry. Ready-to-eat foods, such as deli meats, are expected to be approved in the near future. Not all foods are suitable for this kind of treatment, however. Irradiating raw oysters, for example, damages or kills the live oysters inside the shells and actually decreases their shelf life. Irradiating raw eggs can kill any *Salmonella* inside the shells, but it turns the egg whites milky and makes them more liquid.

Irradiated foods in the supermarket are marked by a symbol called the radura, a flower inside a broken circle. You probably will not find many of them in your local store. People have been slow to accept them, mainly because they do not know or understand what food irradiation is all about.

Irradiation helps to make foods safer, but it should not replace the usual food safety practices. First of all, the more bacteria there are in foods, the more radiation would have to be used—resulting in more changes in taste and nutritional value. Moreover, irradiation—like pasteurization—does not

A microwave oven uses radiation to cook food. It is safe to use a microwave because no radiation is left in the food.

STOPPING SPOILAGE IN OUTER SPACE

Astronauts have been eating irradiated foods since the 1970s. Crews on the space shuttle eat irradiated meat products such as beefsteak and sliced turkey. Steaks, for example, are cooked, packaged in individual pouches, and then irradiated. The treated steaks do not spoil during the spaceflight, even though it may be months before they are eaten. (There are no refrigerators on the spacecraft.)

kill all the microorganisms in foods. New contamination may occur during food handling after the radiation treatment.

Dr. David A. Kessler, a former head of the FDA, says, "Some of us find the idea of irradiated food so frightening that we don't want to believe it's safe. But the fact is, irradiation can make our food supply safer—and that's an important goal."[2] Government agencies will continue to monitor the food supply, helping to keep it safe. Restaurants, delis, and other public eating places are also improving their safety practices. Still, you and your family, as food consumers, have an important role to play. Remember the food safety rules, and you can greatly reduce your risk of getting food poisoning.

FOOD TUNES AIM TO HIT A HEALTHY NOTE

Carl Winter grew up with a love for music. He even joined a band. After finishing college, though, Carl decided to put music behind him and concentrate on a career and family. His college degree was in toxicology, the study of poisons and their effects. After earning a PhD in agricultural and environmental chemistry, he eventually became a college professor at the University of California at Davis. Research on pesticide residues and natural poisons in foods was only part of his work. He was also a talented teacher who knew how to communicate both with his students and with people in the community.

In 1996 Carl brought music back into his life. He had bought a synthesizer, which transformed him into a one-person band, and realized that music could be a powerful tool for getting his message across. Since then he has been writing funny songs about food safety, rewriting the lyrics of popular hits like the Bee Gees' "Stayin' Alive." He has produced several CDs, which have been distributed all over the world. He also goes on twenty-five to thirty tours a year, performing for audiences that include food producers, science teachers, and students from grade school to college age. His programs are a big hit and have earned him nicknames such as the Sinatra of Salmonella, the Elvis of E. coli, and the Artist Formerly Known as Prince of Pesticides.

In writing his songs, Carl draws on his scientific background and also on everyday experiences. A bad chicken dinner at a restaurant while he was touring in Georgia, for example, led to an attack of food poisoning and inspired a new song, "There'll Be a Stomachache Tonight," sung to the tune of the Eagles' hit "Heartache Tonight."[3]

Top 10 Questions and Answers

What is the difference between food poisoning and foodborne illness?

Foodborne illness is a type of food poisoning. Many experts use *foodborne illness* to describe infections caused by microorganisms in food. *Food poisoning* is a more general term that also includes illness due to toxins (poisons) that may occur naturally in foods or may have been introduced from the environment. However, many people use the two terms as synonyms.

I love to eat cold pizza straight out of the refrigerator. Is it safe to eat it cold, or should I heat it up first?

Yes, it's safe if it was put into the refrigerator promptly (within two hours of being cooked) and it has not been there long (less than two days). Bacteria grow quickly at room temperature. Refrigerator temperatures slow down their growth but do not stop it completely. Heating up the pizza will kill most of the bacteria in it, but it will not destroy any toxins they may have produced.

If it is okay to eat rare steak that is still pink inside, then why isn't it safe to eat a rare-cooked hamburger?

A steak is a solid piece of meat. Any contamination with bacteria during handling and food preparation probably occurred only on the outside. These bacteria are killed during cooking, since even a rare steak is still heated to a high temperature on the outside. Hamburger, though, is made of small pieces of chopped meat that are all mixed together when the hamburger patties are formed. The outsides of many of these small pieces wind up inside the hamburger, and if the inside is still pink, they are not cooked well enough to kill bacteria.

If heat kills bacteria in meats, then how do I avoid eating contaminated salads?

You can't heat up salad. First of all, the salad preparer should wash his or her hands. Then the vegetables should be washed thoroughly. The next important thing to remember is not to use the same cutting board or knife that was used to cut up meats, poultry, or seafood so that cross-contamination will not occur.

Am I safer eating at home or at a restaurant?

You have much more control over the food you cook at home, so home cooking is safer. Statistics back this up. In 2014 the Center for Science in the Public Interest reported that restaurants pose twice the risk for food poisoning compared to homes.

My favorite part of baking cookies with my mom is licking the batter afterward. Now I hear that isn't safe. Why?

Cookie batter contains raw eggs, which may carry *Salmonella*. If these bacteria get into your body, you may get food poisoning.

I want to eat a frozen pizza that's in my freezer. Parts of it have freezer burn, though. Is it safe to eat, or should I throw it out?

Foods may get freezer burn if they were not wrapped tightly enough and air gets inside. The air causes chemical changes in the food, which produce leathery, dry spots in the food. Freezer burn will not make you sick, but the food may not taste as good. You can cut those parts away and safely eat what's left.

In my house, we follow the "five-second rule." If you drop a piece of food on the floor and pick it up right away, it's okay to eat. Is it safe to live by the "five-second rule?"

The fact is: When food comes in contact with bacteria, bacteria are transferred to the food almost immediately. Will the food pick up harmful bacteria or enough bacteria to be harmful? It all depends. The bottom line is if you drop food on the floor, you risk having it come in contact with germs.

Is it safe to cut off the moldy part of food and then eat the remainder?

You may have seen the "white dust" on cheddar cheese or fuzzy green spots on bread. While you can see molds on the surface of food, molds can penetrate deep into foods and bacteria can grow along with the mold. Some molds produce allergic reactions and breathing problems. Some are poisonous. With most foods, if they are moldy, throw them out. With a few foods such as hard cheese, hard salami, fruits and vegetables, mold can be cut off and the remainder can be safely eaten.

What do I do when I go picnicking with my family and there is no place to wash my hands?

You can bring along some premoistened towelettes or a hand gel sanitizer that you can buy in any supermarket. These items contain alcohol, which will kill germs on your hands.

TIMELINE OF FOOD POISONING

1600s—Wealthy Americans build icehouses to store their ice and to keep their food frozen.

1790s—Nicolas Appert, a French confectioner, develops the first canning method, by which food can be safely stored in airtight glass bottles for long periods of time.

1793—The first reported outbreak of botulism occurs in Wildbad, Germany, after people eat contaminated blood sausages.

1806—Nicolas Appert tests his canning method on Napoléon's army with positive results.

Early 1800s—The icebox is invented, allowing people to store food inside their homes.

1810—Englishman Peter Durand patents the canning method based on Appert's principles, but he uses cans rather than glass bottles.

1813—Two Englishmen, Bryan Dorkin and John Hall, set up the first commercial canning factory in England.

1829—German physician Justinius Kerner publishes a report describing 230 cases of sausage poisoning.

1857—French chemist Louis Pasteur demonstrates that milk turns sour because microorganisms are growing in it.

1860—Pasteur conducts experiments that use heat to kill microorganisms in beer and wine (pasteurization).

1883—Robert Koch discovers the bacterium that causes cholera.

1885—American scientist Daniel E. Salmon discovers *Salmonella* bacteria.

1895—Belgian physician Emile van Ermengem discovers botulism bacteria.

Late 1800s—The first mechanical refrigerator is invented.

1917—Most major cities in the United States have laws requiring that milk be pasteurized.

1950s—Vernon Brooks discovers that botulinum toxin type A, when injected into a muscle, blocks the release of a messenger chemical from nerves that causes muscles to contract.

1977—Martin Skirrow isolates *Campylobacter jejuni* from patients with diarrhea.

1981—First recorded outbreak of listeriosis in the United States.

1982—First reported food poisoning outbreaks caused by *E. coli* O157:H7 in the United States.

1989—FDA approves BOTOX (botulinum toxin type A) for the treatment of certain eye muscle disorders.

1990—FDA approves the irradiation of poultry.

1994—First human case of infection from mad cow disease is diagnosed.

1997—FDA approves the irradiation of red meat.

2000—FDA approves the irradiation of shell eggs.

2002—First case of vCJD detected in the United States in a woman from the United Kingdom.

2003—Mad cow disease first detected in American cattle.

2006—Outbreaks of *E. coli* O157:H7 traced to packaged spinach; new outbreaks at Taco Bell restaurants.

2009—FDA issues Egg Safety Rule, which establishes requirements for control of *Salmonella enteritidis* in eggs from production through distribution.

2011—FDA Food Safety Modernization Act is signed into law. Shifts focus of regulator from responding to contamination to preventing contamination. Improperly washed cantaloupes kill thirty-three people in the United States.

2013—Foster Farms chickens suspected of making 278 people ill with *Salmonella*.

2014—FDA sets new standards for baby formula, ensuring screening for *Salmonella* and a potentially lethal germ called *Cronobacter*.

Jury convicts peanut plant owner over *Salmonella* outbreak that sickened hundreds.

CDC posts warning about *Listeria* in prepackaged caramel apples.

2015—Contaminated beer kills fifty-six people at funeral in Mozambique.

Chapter Notes

Chapter 1. When Eating Is Risky Business

1. Charles Benson, "Couple complains of food poisoning on Royal Caribbean Cruise," *LawyersandSettlements.com*, November 12, 2009, http://www.lawyersandsettlements.com/features/food_poisoning/foodborne-illness-food-poisoning-4.html#.VPIzny2IadZ.
2. Miriam Falco and Dana Ford, "Royal Caribbean Cruise Cut Short After More than 600 Are Sickened," *CNN.com*, January 27, 2014, http://www.cnn.com/2014/01/26/travel/cruise-ship-illness/.
3. Ben Axelson, "Norovirus Outbreak Forces Royal Caribbean Cruise Ship to Return To Baltimore Early," *Syracuse.com*, February 3, 2015, http://www.syracuse.com/news/index.ssf/2015/02/norovirus_outbreak_baltimore_cruise_ship_grandeur_of_the_seas.html.
4. Centers for Disease Control and Prevention, "Norovirus," *CDC.gov*, accessed February 28, 2015, http://www.cdc.gov/norovirus/about/overview.html.
5. Centers for Disease Control and Prevention, "Estimates of Foodborne Illness in the United States," *CDC.gov*, January 8, 2015, http://www.cdc.gov/foodborneburden.
6. Linda Larsen, "Food Poisoning of the Rich and Famous," *Food Poisoning Bulletin*, January 26, 2012, http://foodpoisoningbulletin.com/2012/food-poisoning-of-the-rich-and-famous/.

Chapter 2. Food Poisoning Through the Ages

1. Judith Walzer Leavitt, *Typhoid Mary: Captive to the Public's Health* (Boston: Beacon Press, 1996), 43.

2. Morton Satin, *Death in the Pot: The Impact of Food Poisoning on History* (Amherst, N.Y.: Prometheus Books, 2007), 166.
3. David E. Barmes, "Health Challenges for Research in the 21st Century," *World Health Organization*, December 6, 2004, http://www.who.int/dg/lee/speeches/2004/barmeslecture/en/.

Chapter 3. Understanding Food Poisoning

1. Pritzker Law, "New Mexico Caramel Apple Listeria Lawsuit Protects Mother and Her Baby Boy," *Food Poisoning Law Blog*, February 7, 2015, http://foodpoisoning.pritzkerlaw.com/archives/cat-caramel-apple-lawsuit.html.
2. Gretchen Goetz, "Jack in the Box *E. coli* Outbreak: Q & A with Brianne Kiner," *BigY*, January 24, 2013, http://www.bigy.com/FoodSafety/CurrentNews/eColiBrianne.
3. Patricia Guthrie, "Aftermath of a Miracle," *The Atlanta Journal*, October 6, 1998, http://www.marlerclark.com/case_news/detail/aftermath-of-a-miracle.
4. Centers for Disease Control and Prevention, "Incidence of Foodborne Illness, 2010," *CDC.gov*, October 3, 2014, http://www.cdc.gov/Features/dsFoodborneIllness/.
5. "Restaurants Pose Double the Risk of Food Poisoning Compared to Homes: Study," *HealthDay*, April 9, 2014, http://consumer.healthday.com/vitamins-and-nutrition-information-27/food-poisoning-news-319/restaurants-pose-double-the-risk-of-food-poisoning-compared-to-homes-study-686681.html.

Chapter 4. How the Trouble Starts

1. Mark Kennedy, "'Why Have They Done This to Her?': Mother Grieved as Bright, Friendly Girl Died the Frightening, Degrading Death that Mad-Cow Disease Brings," *Organic Consumers Association*, June 2, 2001, http://www.organicconsumers.org/madcow/why6201.cfm

2. "CJD Girl Dies at 14," *BBC News*, October 28, 2000, http://news.bbc.co.uk/2/hi/uk_news/995625.stm.
3. Lorraine Fraser, "Millions Watched Zoe's Final Hours," *The Telegraph*, October 29, 2000, http://www.telegraph.co.uk/news/uknews/1372277/Millions-watched-Zoes-final-hours.html; Kennedy.
4. Centers for Disease Control, "Salmonellosis, General Information," *CDC.gov*, November 16, 2009, http://www.cdc.gov/nczved/divisions/dfbmd/diseases/salmonellosis.
5. Ibid.
6. Centers for Disease Control and Prevention, "*Campylobacter*," *CDC.gov*, last modified June 3, 2014, http://www.cdc.gov/nczved/divisions/dfbmd/diseases/campylobacter.
7. The Associated Press, "Farmers Given Sharp Warning Before Outbreak," *MSNBC.com*, September 19, 2006, http://www.msnbc.msn.com/id/14841731; Julia Preston and Carolyn Marshall, "Tainted Spinach Sickens 100 in U.S.," *International Herald Tribune,* September 17, 2006, http://www.iht.com/articles/2006/09/17/news/spinach.php; Associated Press, "Wild Pigs Suspected As Cause of *E. Coli* Outbreak," *MSNBC.com*, October 26, 2006, http://www.msnbc.msn.com/id/15433871/; George Kruchik, "Worst Foodborne Illness Outbreaks in U.S. History," *Healthline,* February 27, 2013, http://www.healthline.com/health-slideshow/worst-foodborne-illness-outbreaks#11.
8. Centers for Disease Control and Prevention, "Campylobacter," CDC.gov, last modified June 3, 2014, http://www.cdc.gov/nczved/divisions/dfbmd/diseases/campylobacter.
9. Centers for Disease Control and Prevention, "Listeria," *CDC.gov,* August 27, 2014, http://www.cdc.gov/listeria/statistics.html.
10. Centers for Disease Control and Prevention, "*E.coli. (Escherichia coli)*," *CDC.gov*, last modified December 1, 2014, http://www.cdc.gov/ecoli/general/index.html/.

11. Centers for Disease Control and Prevention, "*E. coli* O157:H7 and Other Shiga Toxin-Producing *E. coli*," *CDC.gov*, August 5, 2013, http://www.cdc.gov/pulsenet/pathogens/ecoli.html.
12. Illinois Department of Public Health, "*Escherichia coli* O157:H7," *Healthbeat*, accessed February 28, 2015, http://www.idph.state.il.us/public/hb/hbecoli.htm.
13. Centers for Disease Control and Prevention, "Shigella–Shigellosis," *CDC.gov*, August 12, 2014, http://www.cdc.gov/shigella/general-information.html.
14. Centers for Disease Control and Prevention, "Botulism," *CDC.gov*, April 24, 2014, http://www.cdc.gov/nczved/divisions/dfbmd/diseases/botulism/#how_common.
15. Centers for Disease Control and Prevention, "Norovirus: U.S. Trends and Outbreaks," *CDC.gov*, December 30, 2014, http://www.cdc.gov/norovirus/trends-outbreaks.html.
16. Centers for Disease Control and Prevention, "BSE (Bovine Spongiform Encephalopathy, or Mad Cow Disease)," *CDC.gov*, February 19, 2015, http://www.cdc.gov/ncidod/dvrd/bse/.
17. Ibid.
18. Centers for Disease Control and Prevention, "*Vibrio vulnificus*," *CDC.gov*, October 21, 2013, http://www.cdc.gov/vibrio/vibriov.html.
19. Dan Flynn, "Report: Chicken on Menu at 2014 Food Safety Summit was Contaminated," *Food Safety News*, September 25, 2014, http://www.foodsafetynews.com/2014/09/c-perfringens-in-c/#.VPVmzi2IZDW.

Chapter 5. Spotting the Problem and Taking Action

1. Carole Sugarman, "A Taste of Food Poisoning," *The Washington Post*, July 5, 2005, p. HE01, http://www.hepatitisblog.com/hepatitis-a-watch/a-taste-of-food-poisoning/#.VPTd_S2IZDW.
2. Ibid.

Chapter 6. When Good Food Goes Bad

1. Bruce Newman, "Stench From Rotten Refrigerator Sickens 28; San Jose Office Evacuated," *San Jose Mercury News,* May 12, 2009, http://www.mercurynews.com/ci_12351992.

2. Betty Holcomb, "How Safe Is Your Dinner?" *Good Housekeeping,* March 1, 2000, 52.

3. Peter Genovese, "'Sinatra of Salmonella' Sings of Food Safety," *The Star Ledger,* 51, 56.

Glossary

antibiotics—Medicines used to kill bacteria.

antibodies—Special germ-fighting proteins produced by white blood cells.

bacteria—Microscopic organisms that cause harm inside the body when they multiply and produce toxins.

botulism—A type of foodborne illness caused by a toxin produced by the bacterium *Clostridium botulinum*. The toxin attacks the nervous system and can cause muscle weakness, paralysis, and death.

bovine spongiform encephalopathy (BSE)—A rare, deadly disease that affects the brain of cattle; commonly known as mad cow disease. BSE is caused by a defective protein, called a prion, transmitted through contaminated animal feed.

campylobacteriosis—A type of foodborne illness caused by the *Campylobacter jejuni* bacterium.

carrier—A person or animal that is infected with a disease but does not have any symptoms. A carrier can spread the disease-causing germ to others.

cross-contamination—The transfer of microorganisms from one food or person to another. Microorganisms can also be transferred to cutting boards, sponges, and countertops, and then to foods.

dehydration—A removal or severe loss of water. Diarrhea and vomiting can lead to dehydration of the body tissues.

digestive tract—The tubelike passageway inside the body in which food is digested. It extends from the mouth to the anus and includes the esophagus, stomach, and intestines.

disinfectant—Something that kills harmful microorganisms.

drug-resistant bacteria—Bacteria that cannot be killed by an antibiotic.

enzyme—A body chemical that makes reactions go or speeds them up.

feces—Body wastes (undigested food matter and bacteria) formed in the large intestine.

foodborne illness—A sickness caused by consuming food or drink that contains certain kinds of microorganisms that live and grow inside the body; commonly called food poisoning.

fungus (plural fungi)—A plantlike organism that feeds on living or dead matter; includes mushrooms, molds, mildew, and yeasts.

gene—A chemical that carries hereditary information determining a particular trait of an organism.

hemolytic uremic syndrome (HUS)—A complication of *E. coli* O157:H7 infections, especially in young children. Red blood cells are destroyed, which can lead to kidney failure.

host—A living plant or animal that provides food and shelter for another creature.

immune system—The body's disease-fighting system, which includes white blood cells.

incubation period—The period between infection by a disease germ and the onset of symptoms.

inflammation—Redness, heat, and swelling that develop when tissues are damaged.

intestines—Coiled tubelike parts of the digestive tract, in which food is digested and food materials are absorbed.

irradiation—Exposing foods to radiation (high-energy, invisible waves) to kill germs.

lactose intolerance—A condition in which the body is unable to digest lactose, a sugar found in milk and other dairy products.

listeriosis—A type of foodborne illness caused by the bacterium *Listeria monocytogenes*, which can be found in vegetables, milk, cheese, meat, and seafood.

lymph nodes—Small masses of tissue scattered along the lymph system that contain disease-fighting cells.

macrophages—Disease-fighting white blood cells that can eat and digest microorganisms.

microorganisms—Living creatures, such as bacteria, viruses, and parasites, too small to be seen without a microscope.

organic foods—Crops or livestock grown without using pesticides or other chemicals.

pasteurization—A process in which a substance is heated to a very high temperature to kill bacteria, then quickly cooled.

pesticides—Poisonous chemicals used to get rid of insects, weeds, and other pests.

prions—Defective proteins known to cause neurological diseases, such as bovine spongiform encephalopathy (BSE) and Creutzfeldt-Jakob disease.

salmonellosis—A type of foodborne illness caused by one of the *Salmonella* bacteria.

spore—A resting stage of bacteria, covered with a hard, protective coat.

stool—Solid body wastes produced in the intestines; feces.

toxin—A poison.

virus—The smallest kind of microorganism; it cannot even be seen with an ordinary microscope.

white blood cells—Jelly-like blood cells that can move through tissues and are an important part of the body's defenses.

For More Information

Centers for Disease Control and Prevention (CDC) Food Safety

cdc.gov/foodsafety/facts.html

Get facts about foodborne illnesses, track outbreaks, and learn about diagnosis, treatment, and prevention.

National Library of Medicine – MEDLINEplus

nlm.nih.gov/medlineplus

Produced by the National Library of Medicine, this resource provides information about diseases, conditions, and wellness issues in straightforward language.

US Food and Drug Administration (FDA) – Center for Food Safety and Applied Nutrition Outreach and Information Center

fda.gov/Food

This division of the FDA is responsible for the safety of the nation's domestically produced and imported foods. The Web site provides information that includes outbreaks, recalls, packaging, and current research.

US Department of Agriculture (USDA) – Food Safety and Inspection Service

fsis.usda.gov

This public health regulatory agency ensures that America's supply of meat, poultry, and egg products is safe and correctly packaged and labeled. The Web site covers the latest news, regulations and policies, recalls, and the science behind food safety.

Further Reading

Bartos, Judeen. *Food Safety.* San Diego: Greenhaven Press, 2011.

Hillstrom, Laurie. *Food Regulations and Safety.* San Diego: Lucent Books, 2012.

Lew, Kristi. *Food Poisoning: E. Coli and the Food Supply*. New York: Rosen, 2011.

Nakaya, Andrea. *Food-Borne Illnesses*. San Diego: Reference Point Press, 2011.

Perrett, Heli. *The Safe Food Handbook*. New York: The Experiment, 2011.

INDEX